A Return to Emptiness

A Return to Emptiness

Stories by

CHRIS RANSICK

CONUN
DRUM
bɹEZZ

CONUNDRUM PRESS
A Division of Samizdat Publishing Group, LLC.

A Return to Emptiness. Copyright © 2012 by Chris Ransick.

ISBN: 978-0-9713678-6-9

Library of Congress Cataloging-in-Publication Data is available upon request.

Some of these stories have been published in *California Quarterly, Hard Ground: Writing the Rockies, Pittsburgh Quartlery,* and *Element.*

Conundrum Press books may be purchased with bulk discounts for educational, business, or sales promotional use. For information please email: info@conundrum-press.com

Conundrum Press online: conundrum-press.com

for Jean Ransick
because some gifts
come back to you

Contents

Foreword

The work was straightforward, and seemingly simple enough: read and edit my previously published collection of short fiction for a new edition. I had done this for a new edition of my first book, *Never Summer*, and learned the challenge is to smooth the obvious failures of diction and expression but to leave the essence of the book alone. I have read most of these stories to audiences, some many times, but when I came to them as a distanced editor, it was neither desirable nor possible to re-inhabit the author who wrote the earliest drafts more twenty years ago. This affirms a central truth of the writing life—time and experience change our very language, cadence of speech, patterns of imagery, and sensibilities.

A bare few paragraphs into the first story I had the odd sensation of entering a literary hall of mirrors, angled shards of glass refracting characters in parts and pieces, beyond my ability to touch them, to change their trajectories. I know how intimately I once imagined them into print but in being fixed there, they had escaped me. The authorial voice, whatever (or whether) that is, sounded familiar but extraneous. Here was a style in which I no longer write, sentences penned by an other-author. How well this graphs the *implied author*, a persona that masks the actual human being operating the keyboard. I know the rooms in which these stories were written and can recall how the afternoon light hit the writing desk as the sounds of playing children spilled through the open windows. Those children are grown now, and so is that author. Like any reader of fiction, I get only a version of author a given story *implies*. This displacement is both vaguely disturbing and wholly intriguing. It's a a hot June afternoon on the Front Range of Colorado, I'm a long way down the road I chose, and these stories now move beyond my reach, fractal whorls of memory and imagination. I'm gratified to visit this hall and I have restrained myself. I have only polished the glass.

I wrote *A Return to Emptiness* in the decade that followed the death of my father, Jack Ransick. It seemed the thing to do. I was simultaneously writing the poems in *Never Summer*, so those books serve as a fiction/poetry *Pa Kua* of creative response, gathered on journeys and in residence around the American west, drafted in notebooks and finished at a desk on Pearl Street. The characters and plots here are imagined but the landscapes, never. I built them from observation, as in a poem. No son loses a father in these stories, though the people here surely do lose—and find—other things. Loss is common to us all, yet multifarious in individual experience. I wrote these stories not primarily to describe loss but to circumscribe it—which is to say that I drew a circle of narratives round the experience to both locate and *limit* it. I was vaguely aware of this at the time of the writing. It's quite clear now.

Nobody gets out of this life without experiencing loss, as well as what is offered in recompense to those with the humility and quietude to accept emptiness. Stories are an ancient way of communicating experience and a collection of short fiction is a unique and complex symbol set that can, in the best cases, fill a void, turn loss to gain. If I had my way, this book would do that for the reader. There's more to say about all this but it is better conveyed by the stories themselves. I've relished the opportunity to travel back in time, lean over the author's shoulder where he's writing in the morning before work, tell him what he already knows—things balance. Except when they don't, and for that we have stories.

—C.R.

Denver, June 2012

But I think something else—a reverence that disavows keeping things—must come to us all, sooner or later.

—Mary Oliver, *Blue Pastures*

A Return to Emptiness

Rachael shook her head to ward off sleep and rolled down the window. Cool air carried the pungent scent of sagebrush over her and for the moment she felt revived. Her aged Dodge sedan settled in at seventy miles an hour, aimed at the fringe of pink bleeding upward in advance of the sun. Soon enough the plains would begin to swelter, the hard yellow light of a summer morning banishing everything subtle.

You could never say such a place was empty, she thought. Rachael had made that mistake the first time she had come to Wyoming several years before. It had been late winter. The hard light of the sun on wind-scoured contours passed for a summer landscape as long as she kept the car heat on high and ignored the pockets of snow crouching in blue shade behind low protrusions of rock.

Her sister had been sitting in the passenger seat during that trip, and as if reading Rachael's mind, she began suddenly to name things: high desert plants, mammals, birds of prey, cloud formations, the geologic terms for exposed rock, the Indian names of mountain ranges breaching the plains in the distance.

"You know," Jenna had said when she finished her recitation, "it might help if you stopped the car and got out." So Rachael had pulled over. They climbed the barbed wire fence, and walked toward a small butte in the distance. At one point they came across the desiccated body of a lamb lying amid the rocks, and later, as they sat on the earth near the foot of the butte, Rachael felt the wind whipping her loose hair in a dance around her. The quieter they became, the more life emerged from the landscape around them. The lesson was brief and simple. In that moment, it had become possible that she might see this place as Jenna saw it.

Rachael wondered again what had made Jenna stay, although she knew the answer—had known it since the first time she heard her sister had taken up residence in a dilapidated sheep trailer on the edge of a sprawling ranch that hadn't been worked in decades. That was almost ten years ago, and some things had changed since, including her sister's relocation to a well-kept cabin on sixty acres of her own land. Jenna never said where the money had come from and Rachael never asked. What hadn't changed was Jenna's need for isolation. She called it "immersion." It had first brought her here, and it kept her in a place where so many people passed through, convinced that the land was, finally, empty.

Rachael had come to know her sister through her letters, which came in a rush at first but more sparingly toward the end. They were infused with poetry and philosophy and the voice seemed too calm to be coming from a place inside her sister that before had harbored violent storms. Rachael didn't understand the change fully because she hadn't been close to her sister before Jenna left home. For years they had shared little except an unspoken knowledge about their mother, who in her pain and rage had kept everyone in a constant state of withdrawal. Jenna had left suddenly, with no good-byes, but almost immediately she began sending Rachael envelopes stuffed with dried desert plants she labeled with their local names and lore. Sometimes there were only twigs of aromatic sagebrush or dried blooms, but once, neatly packed in a box of tissue, was the rattle from a small diamondback.

Rachael saw in these letters what had been lost between them, and what they might yet recover. Making this trip now was the best chance she would have to recover anything at all.

The sun had come up and soon the air grew hot, blasting in through the open car window. There were only twenty miles left to go before the turnoff, and Rachael planned to stop for breakfast. Her bladder ached—damned roadhouse coffee, and too much of it, she thought—and the gas gauge was leaning on empty.

Rachael pulled off at the first, and only, opportunity she had. The two-lane highway had no signs posted to designate services available ahead, just one indicating the required drop in the speed limit to fifty miles per hour. The sign had a jagged hole blown through the center of the zero. Good shot, she thought to herself as she applied gentle pressure to the brake and coasted toward the gravel lot outside a small diner. A woman was just opening the front door from the inside. The woman didn't smile, but with a slight nod of her head she seemed to say that yes, breakfast was being served. Rachael cut the engine, recognizing this as a place Jenna once described in a letter—a knot of low buildings back from the highway, just a diner and gas station at the edge of the pavement.

* * *

The food was good and the woman had been quick to her table with fresh, hot coffee. Rachael wondered how many mornings the woman had made the coffee, only to drink it herself. Don't assume emptiness, she heard a voice say in her head. There must be people who daily traveled the road and frequently stopped for coffee or a meal. She looked around the room at the walls, decorated with framed paintings of mountain ranges, and not surprisingly, one featuring a weary horse carrying its equally weary rider along a line of fence posts sticking up through drifted snow. Rachael could see the wind moving through the frame and knew the artist must himself be the man on the horse, and he had painted this self-portrait accurately, from grooved memory. As she looked around, her eye snagged on a patch of black and white photos behind the cash register and she wondered about the people in the pictures, wondered how long ago the shutter had captured their faint smiles.

The woman saw Rachael staring and came across the room toward her. She refilled her coffee cup, the rich smell wafting up. It reminded Rachael how hungry she had grown as she crossed the vast, black plain all night.

"Tired?" the woman asked.

Rachael nodded.

"Driving all night will do that to you, especially if you're on your own. You ought to try a traveling partner if you can manage it."

"I could have used some help with the driving," Rachael agreed, and her own voice sounded far off to her. "I thought I was seeing things there for a while. At one point I thought I saw a ghost run across the highway, a woman in a long white dress, and then later I know I saw a billboard somewhere, all lit up, with a huge cowboy on it. I saw the lights from way off and couldn't tell what it was for the longest time."

"That would be outside Douglas," the woman said, but as she spoke, something across the room distracted her. Rachael could tell someone had appeared in the doorway but she didn't look back. Instead her eye was drawn to the woman's arm, to a spot just above her wrist. A blue-green butterfly no bigger than a nickel was tattooed there, and Rachael, who was not usually moved by tattoos, found this one beautiful. She took a sip of coffee and before she could stop herself, she asked the question she'd been rehearsing all night.

"I'm heading toward Kaycee," she said. "It's in the direction of where my sister used to live. I wonder if you might have known her—Jenna McPherson?"

"You talk about her as if she were dead," the woman said.

Her head spun for a moment and then she caught the woman's gaze. "She is," Rachael said. "I meant to say that. She died in a car accident in April, not far from here."

The woman's eyes flickered. Rachael thought this woman must certainly know of accidents that occur along this two lane. There must have been many over the years. She must know the details of some, sad stories of travelers and the sadder ones involving young boys out drinking or an elderly couple from a nearby town.

"I guess I did hear about that," the woman said. "She was young, wasn't she?"

"She was twenty-nine," Rachael said.

"Yes, I heard about that. Your sister. I'm sorry." She wiped the table down with a wet cloth and seemed as if she would keep talking, but she did not.

Rachael took another sip of her coffee. "Can you tell me what you know about it? Anything, really, would be helpful."

"There isn't much to tell," the woman said. Rachael waited for her to continue, and for the first time felt afraid to find out what had really happened to her sister.

"Do you know how the accident happened?" she asked again.

The woman shook her head. "Nobody knows much, just

that it happened past midnight. The car ended up in a dry wash alongside the highway just west of here."

"Did they determine who was driving—my sister or the man she was with?"

The woman looked puzzled, and then, Rachael thought, almost angry. "Didn't they tell you that much?" she asked. "Didn't they tell you who was driving?"

Rachael shook her head. "I didn't have a very good source," she said. "My mother isn't well."

"It wasn't your sister driving," the woman said.

Rachael paused, wanting a moment to consider this new information, but she also wanted to ask another question before the woman left her alone again. "Did you know who my sister was with?"

The woman didn't answer immediately. When she did, her voice had changed, grown cold again. "I know of his family. He came in here occasionally. The name was Tom Corcoran," she said and topped off Rachael's coffee cup. "The family has a ranch not far from here." Rachael thought she saw the woman look up again, past her shoulder, before she continued. "I'm sorry about your sister," she said, and then she turned away and went back to the kitchen at the rear of the diner.

* * *

The sun burned brighter than ever. Rachael stood just outside the diner and squinted across the parking lot toward her car, engulfed in glare. She put on her sunglasses and waited for her eyes to adjust.

As they did, Rachael saw a child and she knew it was the person she had sensed earlier, hovering at the edge of the woman's vision. The child leaned against the front bumper of her car as if waiting for her. Rachael walked slowly across the gravel of the lot, her thin-soled shoes registering the rough surface. She couldn't tell if it was a boy or a girl until she got closer and glimpsed the hair, black and thick, gathered in a loose ponytail. The girl wore a pair of dirty jeans, an old orange T-shirt, and sneakers without socks. She was staring at Rachael with great interest. Rachael judged her to be about twelve years old.

"Hello," Rachael said. The girl said nothing at first, just cocked her head slightly and ran her fingertips over the fender of the car, studying Rachael's face as she did.

Rachael smiled politely and opened the door to get in.

"You're her sister, aren't you?" the girl asked suddenly. Her voice was husky, but came almost in a whisper that seemed lost in the gathering heat and dust stirred up by the wind.

The girl's question stopped Rachael. "Whose sister?" she said, more as a reflex than anything else. But she understood, even as the words left her lips, that this girl must have known Jenna.

"You look just like her," the girl said. "Except her hair was sort of red. In this kind of sun, it would definitely look red."

Who was this girl? Rachael took in her bronze skin, windburnished and smooth. Her eyes were dark brown. A pretty child, Rachael thought, though she noticed the long limbs, the pants too short in the leg, and was reminded of the awkward time when she had put on growth fast, in surges.

"I know where it happened," the girl said, and the air grew electric between the two of them. Rachael understood what the girl meant. She knew where the car had gone off the road, the place Jenna had died. "I can show you where."

Rachael smiled again. "Your mother would hardly approve of you getting in the car with a stranger and driving off down the road. Besides, maybe if you give me good directions I can find the place myself."

The girl shook her head. "You'd never find it. It's not like it's marked or anything—you know how some people put up those little white crosses. I saw one road once, up near Browning by the Blackfeet Reservation, and there were about a hundred of them. It's not marked like that, but I know the place. I've been there. We could go. And anyway," the girl said, nodding in the direction of the diner, "she ain't my momma."

* * *

The heat of the day was rising faster now. A hot wind surged against the car as it crested small rises in the road. Rachael looked across at the girl, hunkered down in the passenger seat with the seat belt pulled across her thin hips. She thought about what the woman in the diner had said when she'd gone back in to ask permission to take the girl as a guide to point out the scene of the accident. The woman had laughed a tight and bitter laugh as she poured another pot of water into the top of the coffee machine.

"No, the girl's not mine. She just hangs around here, and I feed her most of the time. Lea Johnson keeps her, or I guess I should say there's a bed at her house for the girl. But she doesn't always use it. Sometimes she sleeps here, on one of the bench seats along the wall. I keep a blanket around."

The woman had put the empty pot beneath the spout and turned to face Rachael. A light sweat hung about her face and a lock of hair had broken loose and dangled down over her brow. She brushed it away with the back of her hand. "The girl has only been here since last August. She said—and I had to ask her quite a few times before she told me because the child doesn't talk much—she said it was the fifth house she'd been placed in, that she could recall, anyway. I knew I'd never find out why she got moved around so much, but I expect she won't

be here long, either. Things aren't working out. Lea knows
she's down here with me mostly, and she doesn't care. She
doesn't look after the child properly. I expect one day somebody will come and take her off that woman's hands."

"I'll bring her back here straight away," Rachael said. "I don't
intend to linger at the site. I just want to see where it happened."

"The girl knows the spot," the woman said. "I know you
won't do her any harm, and besides, my OK is as good as anyone's."

"Thanks," Rachael said. The woman nodded. "By the way,
what's her name?"

"Maya." The woman looked past Rachael to the door, where
the squares of sunlight cast on the tile floor through the windows were ridged by a small, flickering shadow on one side, a
shadow that withdrew as Rachael followed the woman's gaze.

"They were real close, you know," the woman said, more
quietly.

"The girl . . . and my sister?"

"Yeah. And I should tell you, I did know Jenna." When she
said this, she lowered her eyes for a moment to avoid Rachael's
gaze. "I'm sorry I didn't say it before. It's just that she was a
very private person. I could tell that much, and I respected it.
We talked a bit but she never said a word about having a sister,
or about the rest of her family." The woman explained how
Maya had been helping her one busy Sunday morning by serving up plates when Jenna had come in. The girl didn't return to
the kitchen after taking out an order to Jenna. "That's when I
heard her laughing," the woman said. "I came around front to
check on her and she was sitting across the booth from Jenna,
eating the toast that had come with the meal and laughing at
something your sister had said. I'd never heard the child laugh

before," the woman said. "Jenna came in to the diner more often after that, and Maya was always there to share her breakfast when she did. Sometimes they would leave together and be gone the whole day. The girl was much better off with her than hanging around at Lea's place."

There was a momentary pause, and then the woman looked up into Rachael's face. "I don't mean any disrespect," she said, "but why'd it take you so long to get here? I mean, the accident happened over two months ago. How come nobody from the family showed up until now?"

Rachael sensed the girl listening again at the door. "It was because of my mother," she finally said. "She didn't tell me what had happened until last week." Rachael saw the puzzled look on the woman's face. "It's a long story. I came as soon as I found out."

The woman considered this a moment, and then taking the damp towel from her shoulder, she began to clean the table in front of her. Without looking up she said, "Maya will show you the place."

* * *

So now the girl was sitting in the front seat of Rachael's car, gazing straight ahead as they drove the gently sloping highway. Rachael tried to talk with her, draw her out a little in the first few minutes, but the girl only murmured short replies. She seemed to be concentrating on a point beyond the horizon that drew all her attention. They had driven only about fifteen miles when suddenly the girl lifted up her head and reached across to tap Rachael on the arm.

"There," she said, "see it?" She was pointing off to the right shoulder, and Rachael thought they had come unexpectedly upon the site of the accident, much closer to the diner than the woman indicated.

"Is this the place?" she asked. She pulled off the highway, spotting a dirt road that went over a cattle guard. It was one of the only gaps she'd seen in the barbed wire that ran along the miles of highway.

"This isn't where she died," Maya said, and Rachael could not grasp the emotion in her voice, wavering there just beyond detection. "Just go up this dirt road a ways," the girl said. "I've got to show you something else."

Rachael looked down the road. It ran in a wide arc around a sage-dotted butte about a half-mile away and then disappeared behind it. As she eased the car over the cattle guard, the rough clatter of her loose front end suspension reminded her how hard a washboard road could be on her old car. The girl seemed more animated now, and turning to look at her, Rachael realized she had no idea where she was being led or what was going on in the girl's head. "How far up this road?" she asked, slowing down further as the car skittered sideways over ripples on the packed dirt, kicking up a wall of dust that blew thickly across the land behind them.

"Not far. I'll show you."

* * *

They drove a half-hour on the dirt road. It took all Rachael's skill to straddle the eroded gullies that grew wider and more frequent. She scraped bottom several times, and though she was curious about going on, she also wanted to make sure she could get back from wherever it was they were going. Just as she was deciding to find a place to pull off and turn around, they crested a small rise and the horizon dropped away sharply before them.

She had never seen anything like it before. Moments earlier she'd been staring across what had seemed an interminable, rolling desert of sagebrush and red dirt, broken only by strange, globular rock outcrops and an occasional low butte. Suddenly a wide gash in the land yawned before the hood of the car, a canyon a quarter mile across, its bottom lost in green brush. The girl sat up in her seat and leaned forward to look out over the dash. For the first time Rachael saw a smile tilt the corner of her mouth, and then it was gone again.

"What is this place?" she asked the girl.

"It's the canyon," Maya said.

Rachael first felt a wave of frustration, but as she looked again at the gorge she felt that sensation washing away. After a moment she cut the motor. The girl undid her seat belt, opened the door, and climbed out. She walked out in front of the car and went about a dozen paces before stopping and turning to face Rachael, who had remained in her seat.

"Aren't you coming?" she said, her voice thin as a cloud evaporating in dry summer sky.

They walked nearly a mile along the canyon's lip. The road did continue, zigging along the rim of the canyon, but the gullies were so wide and filled with rocks that Rachael knew her car would have become hopelessly stuck had she proceeded. The girl walked ahead, saying nothing, and Rachael followed, content to trust that this would somehow fit in the story of Jenna's life she was piecing together.

Then, suddenly, there was no more road at all before them. It came to an abrupt end and the canyon opened out into a broad arc, the red-browns of the surrounding plain giving way to deeper and deeper green as the walls descended and converged on a ribbon of pale water looping along the bottom. Rachel knew it would take all afternoon to climb down, if that were possible at all, and longer to get back up.

"I didn't want to take you to where the wreck happened,"

Maya said. "I know where it is. I could have shown you. I still can if you want. But I wanted to come here first." The girl's black hair had come loose from the ponytail and was blowing across her face, a few strands catching in the moist corners of her mouth. Her eyes, hard and dark, scanned Rachael's face. She sat down then, her legs dangling over the rock ledge.

Rachael took her place beside the girl and stared out across the canyon to the other side. Halfway down the opposite cliff wall a large cave mouth gaped at them, and she saw a thin trail leading from it down to the river below.

"Jenna used to bring you here, didn't she?" Rachael asked

The girl nodded, and held her gaze across the canyon.

"Did you used to sit here, at this place?"

"We sat here sometimes, and down a ways, on that big rock that hangs over the edge. Once we went down to the river. It took all day and we didn't get back until dark. That was the only time we ever stayed out all night," Maya said. "We slept in the car. Jenna had some crackers and soda in the trunk. We snuggled up in the back seat so we weren't cold."

Rachael laughed. She could see her sister scuffling down the steep, rocky slope, her jeans dusty where she'd used her backside as a brake. She tried to imagine Jenna curled up in the car, eating a simple meal with this strange, sad girl as the stars grew brilliant in the sky above them and the last light faded from the rim to the west.

"You were good friends," Rachael said, "you and Jenna."

"We were good friends," the girl echoed. After a pause she said, "I never had anybody like her. Never before."

For the first time since she'd heard about the accident, Rachael missed Jenna—not the far off, hollow feeling she'd had when her mother finally told her what had happened, but a hard ache that throbbed inside her chest. Almost by instinct, she scooted closer to Maya and put her arm around the girl's shoulder, bony like a boy's and warm under her thin shirt. The girl shuddered slightly, and they bent into the gusts of wind that came stronger now.

"For a while, I thought it wasn't true, and that she'd come back," Maya said. "I thought maybe it was just a bad accident, and nobody could tell who'd been in the car, and maybe it was just another car like hers. I never had called her before on the phone, and so I got some coins and tried to see if the operator had a number for her, but anyway, I didn't know her last name." The girl paused here. "What is your last name?"

"McPherson," Rachael said.

The girl nodded her head. "I didn't ever think to ask her. It doesn't matter. She probably didn't have a phone at her place anyway." Maya stood up, picked up a rock and let it fly out over the canyon, listening for the soft thud when it hit. "I guess I really knew Jenna was dead as soon as I heard about it. I just didn't want to believe it. I was listening to some people talk at the diner because I always do that—and they were saying it was the woman who lived out alone on the old Mickelson ranch, and then I knew it was her for sure, the way they were talking about her. I got Lea's boyfriend to take me out to where it happened."

Then the girl turned again and looked at her, and put her small hand on Rachael's. "It's nothing personal, but you know, they didn't much like her. People around here are like that. They don't trust anybody that isn't born and raised here. I know that. We both did. Jenna and me were the same that way. But I could see Jenna wasn't anybody to be afraid of, and besides, she didn't care what people thought about her."

"I know," Rachael said. The girl looked at her for a moment, and then away.

"She told me not to mind, either," Maya said. "I always knew I shouldn't care about what other kids say to me, but it's not ever easy to just ignore it. But when Jenna told me about herself, it was easier. I felt different after that. She used to tell me all about the desert, things I never heard from anybody else, and it was almost like she'd lived here longer than any of them, knew more about this place. And she could talk to me about personal things, she knew how I felt." Maya stopped short, and looked down over the canyon rim.

Rachael gave her the moment to herself. She watched a bank of dark grey clouds sliding in from the south and massing, tufts of moisture trailing out of the bottom edge and evaporating before they reached the hard, baked plain beneath.

"You're a lot like your sister," the girl said. "You might not think so, but I can tell you are."

The words caught Rachael off guard. Maybe it was true after all. It was a kind thing Maya had just said, a truth she couldn't verify but that she could accept.

"Thank you," Rachael said. "Thank you for bringing me here."

* * *

They sat on the rim of the canyon until late afternoon, when the wind finally grew calm, then hiked back to the car. Rachael eased it back over the dirt road and when they reached the highway she hesitated before putting on her left turn blinker and letting it click. Maya stared silently out her window. There wasn't a car within miles but Rachael took her time turning out onto the pavement, heading back toward the diner.

After a moment, the girl spoke again without looking at her. "Don't you want to see the place?" she asked.

Rachael shook her head. "I already have."

They drove the rest of the way in silence, and Rachael kept the speed down like she had not done since hitting the Wyoming border. When she pulled up at the diner it was nearly dark. The lights inside were low and a closed sign hung on the door, which was slightly ajar. She slowed to a halt and cut the engine. Maya sat a moment in the car, and Rachael thought she saw a shadow behind one of the curtained windows, moving slightly. Maya undid her seat belt but she didn't get up right away. When she did, she leaned over and kissed Rachael on the cheek, a touch so light Rachael wasn't sure the girl's lips had actually brushed against her skin. Before Rachael could turn to look at her, she was out the door and moving across the gravel toward the diner.

The Pepper Plant

Carl realized one autumn afternoon, as a sunbeam fell across his dusty desk and onto his calendar, that he'd forgotten to turn the page and the month of October was already two weeks old. This bothered him intensely. It was not the sort of thing he usually overlooked. He rose from his chair, retrieved the calendar, and turned the page, expecting to feel a sense of calm and order again as he sat down.

Instead, his chair rocked beneath him. He put his feet down and shifted his weight. The chair rocked again, just a bit. His chair had always stood perfectly flat before.

"Ginny," he called out, "has this chair ever rocked a bit on you?" Moments later a slender, red-haired woman appeared in the doorway of the room. She grinned at him, and as he looked into her brown eyes he could count there every year of their long companionship.

"No," she said in a soft voice. "It sits flat for me, but then I don't weigh as much as you."

"I swear it wasn't like this yesterday," Carl said. "Maybe a leg is loose." He rose again and lifted the chair, examining the sturdy oak legs and supports. He ran his hand over the chipped wood, checking the joints, but he could find nothing that seemed loose. Carl set the chair back down, rocked it to gauge which leg might be off, and tried it on several spots along the floor. Finally he sat down again. He meant to say how strange it was but when he looked up, Ginny was no longer in the doorway. He rocked forward again in the chair. This time the tilt was more pronounced.

The sunlight pouring through his study window dimmed suddenly as a thick bank of clouds passed across the sky. Carl looked out at the ruins of their summer garden. Once-verdant plants draped blasted limbs and tendrils over cage and trellis, a few puckered tomatoes, cucumbers, and peppers dangling in a faint wind.

Carl looked again at the calendar and noticed Halloween fell on a Friday. The last year he and Ginny had gone to a rollicking party dressed as skate punks. Carl had put a dozen mock earrings in his lower lip and combed his hair in front of his face. Ginny had slung a pair of his oversized jeans low on her hips and pinned them to a pair of boxers that she cinched at her waist. Their best friends, Linda and Spencer, had come as Joan of Arc and Merlin. Lots of people came in costumes, and then there were all the rest who dressed in solid black. What a party it had been, Carl thought. He remembered how, afterwards, Ginny had backed him up against a stone wall that marked the west side of the graveyard. She had gotten a good grip on him and said, "If we have to walk home, let's take the back route."

Yes, that had been one scary night. He'd found leaves in his coat pockets the next day and had to move gingerly due to a curious abrasion on his back.

The memory faded, and Carl looked again at the calendar before him. Something about it still bugged him, and after a moment it dawned on him. Last year, Halloween had been a Friday night, too. He remembered leaving work, closing the shop doors for the weekend, hearing the crush of people on the street and thinking to himself how alive the night was. Crisp air had carried sounds of laughter, cars going fast, the clanging of delivery doors, and the savory aroma of the Greek restaurant next door.

That had been a year ago, and he was sure it had been a Friday night. All year long, Carl turned the many other calendars in his life, always on time, always finding the days in order. His watches had all turned on time—no batteries had run out all year. However, one night a storm knocked out electrical power, and so he'd had to reset his alarm, the microwave, and the stove. Carl liked to maintain order and he'd been diligent the whole year through, but nothing explained this.

Carl confirmed that it hadn't been a leap year. He looked again at his calendar and saw it listed October as only thirty days long. There was no thirty-first of October. Printer's error, he thought to himself, and he felt the urge to turn the page and see what November looked like. He reached his hand out and then remembered what a friend had told him recently: "Don't get ahead of yourself, Carl. It isn't healthy." Instead, he picked up a marker and wrote '31' on the open box next to October 30.

"What should we have for dinner tonight?" Ginny asked him. He hadn't known she was back. In fact, when he turned it looked like she had never left. She was standing in the same casual way, leaning against the door frame, wisps of black hair falling loose from a comb at the nape of her neck. He noticed for the first time how much fuller her figure seemed these days, her waist curving into strong hips and thighs.

Then he realized it wasn't Ginny.

Carl cleared his throat. "Dinner," he said. "I don't know."

"I could make something up," she said. "What sounds good?"

Carl was quiet for a moment. He felt his pulse race. Then he said, "Who are you?"

"Very funny," she said, laughing. "I guess I'll just figure out dinner myself."

She turned and went back toward the kitchen, and in a moment there came the sounds of water running and things being chopped. Carl rose to follow her but then thought better of the idea and stood watching out the window as the sun broke through again. It fell on a pepper plant he hadn't noticed before, one that seemed to have survived the frost. Its leaves were still deep green and two or three branches were heavy with ripe yellow fruit.

"Carl," Ginny's voice called from the kitchen. "Can you get me some fresh tomatoes from the garden?" It was Ginny's voice, although just a shade deeper and a little husky. Carl got up from the chair, which rocked back behind him a full inch. He put his jacket on, went out the back door, and walked into the yard. The air was chill but the brilliant sun felt warm on his skin and he stood a long moment with his eyes closed, letting the rays fall on his face.

Carl wasn't sure what was happening, but he could think of no other thing to do than to walk toward the garden. He let the gate swing shut behind him and looked toward that one pepper plant, still green with healthy fruit on its limbs. Everything else was blasted. He wondered at the scene before him, making a note to plant this variety of pepper again the coming spring. Then he reached out and picked several of the long yellow peppers and slipped them into his pocket.

The tomatoes at the garden's far end were goners. Those that remained were maimed and shrunken, black spots along their skin. The vines had gone brown and tough, and they clung to the cage supports like ancient crones approaching another long winter. He went back toward the house, but stopped short, unsure whether he ought to actually go inside.

He thought about this all the way up the porch, into the hall, and toward the kitchen door. There really was no escaping it, and so taking a deep breath, Carl walked in.

Ginny was at the stove. She turned and looked at him, smiled and shook her head, and went back to her task. He wanted to go to her, put his hand along her familiar side, bury his face in her golden locks and just hold her. "Bring those over here, will you already?" she said.

Carl reached into his pocket and brought out three tomatoes, deep red, aromatic, heavy with juice. He walked over, drinking in the hearty aromas of sautéed garlic and herbs. He put the tomatoes on the counter near the cutting board, his hands shaking noticeably.

"You're a very nice man," Ginny said, and turning to him, she pulled Carl against her swollen belly and kissed him deep and slow. "You're going to make a wonderful father."

She pressed against his lips again, her body hot beneath the touch of his chilled fingers, and looking over her shoulder, Carl saw the clock on the microwave blink and go dark.

The Boy Disappeared

David fell asleep on the couch. He had decided to watch the local news, figuring it was unlikely rescue workers had found the boy's body but wanting to know just the same. The brief report had turned out to be nothing more than a couple of clipped interviews with a police officer and an eyewitness, interspersed with shots of the jagged hole in the ice gaping behind the reporter. The reporter was stuck on the word "shock," returning to it several times as he stood shivering in the glare of the camera lights, his face pinched with cold.

"The boy is still missing," the officer had said. David recognized him as the senior officer who was arriving at the accident scene just as David was leaving.

"Will the search continue through the night?" the reporter asked.

The officer shook his head. "We're calling off the search until daylight." It was clear rescue workers knew little more than they had when David filed his story and left the newspaper an hour earlier.

David watched another news report about a woman near Seattle who had survived when her parachute failed to open completely and she landed in a reservoir east of the city. It reminded him of how at work, when things got slow in the evenings, he would browse the AP wire at the newspaper, reading details about accidents like that from every region of the world. The disaster file was always full, the updates frequent. The story of this boy, his story, would make it onto the wire and from there into the corners and nooks of papers scattered here and there. He thought about this and felt vaguely ashamed. He wondered whether people would linger in the morning over what he'd written—the story of a boy disappearing through a hole in a shelf of river ice.

David's phone rang and he jumped, his heart banging against his ribs. He clicked off the television and moved to pick up the receiver, but after a moment, he thought better of it. All he wanted now was to sleep, to rest and forget the day. He could guess who it was, anyway—Lemke calling to check an insignificant detail on his story before it went to press. No doubt Lemke had been watching the broadcast and heard something he thought was crucial, something David had missed. "Go to hell," he said aloud. Then he lay back on the couch, stuffing his feet down under the afghan, and let the phone go, counting the rings until it stopped. Then it started ringing again. This happened several times. Nobody else but Lemke would do that.

David had stood all afternoon in a hard February cold that clung to the riverbank. His neck was stiff and he couldn't get comfortable now. He lay in the darkness of his front room, headlights of passing cars cascading down his walls, and closed his eyes again. Images from that afternoon flickered on the backs of his eyelids, scenes of people gathered along the riverbank in the hours that followed the accident. They stood in small knots, one or another of them occasionally stepping

away to converse with someone or to stand for a while at
the edge of the ice before returning to the group. What did
they expect to see, David wondered. Why were they hanging
around? But he knew the answers. They were following the
same impulses that would cause them to pick up the paper the
next morning, the curiosity that drew him to the disaster file
in the evenings when the newsroom grew silent and deserted.

The sheriff's rescue unit had been called in after initial
rescue attempts. They worked furiously, breaking up the ice
downstream, hoping the frigid temperatures of the water
would preserve the chance to resuscitate the boy. They even
brought in an old man named Solomon Finley who fished the
river in that spot daily during the warm months. They hoped
he could point out places where the body might have wedged
up against a sandbar. The old man walked the ice with them;
workers tore at the ice downstream with the blunt sides of axes,
some falling into the water and having to be hauled out themselves.

The light faded early, and with the lowering darkness the
faces of rescue workers registered a subtle despair. Finally, no
one had been able to do a thing except stare across the ice to
the opening where the boy had gone in. Water flowed fast and
black underneath the narrow gash. David remembered thinking it was too small to admit a human body, even that of a boy.

He was unable now to sleep, and so David lay on his dilapidated couch and wondered what must it have been like to feel
the crust give way. He imagined slipping down into the terrible water, first the shock of cold and then the current pulling,
his hands groping for a solid thing to anchor him. What must
it have been like to be pulled away from the slit of light above?

David had covered the police beat for two years. Accidents
and disasters were his regular material. It was worst in the

summer, when drunken teenage kids from the Bitterroot Valley tried to navigate Highway 93. There were frequent single-car accidents. More often than not the police found the empty cans and bottles scattered about the scene. There were other seasonal disasters too, such as the ill-fated party of three hunters who went out one morning in late November, elk tags on their packs. They had ignored the late reports of a fast-moving storm descending out of Canada and they paid the price for it. One straggled up to the back porch of a ranch house three days later, frostbitten, snow-blind, and unable to speak for hours. When he did finally come around he could tell them nothing about where his two partners were. They had separated in a white-out. The second hunter was found dead several days later. The third, David knew, would probably show up when the snow melted in May.

Newspaper people seemed to grow callous from all their exposure to disaster, to the horrifying and absurd details of how people suffered and died. In the newsroom, there were often uncomfortable jokes made about the miserable and entirely predictable surge of domestic violence that always accompanied the closing weeks of winter. Lemke was big on covering that, and David could never laugh off the things he said. It was his beat, and David learned more about the beatings and shootings than anybody. He knew he'd find an escalating number of terrorized women and kids in the police reports each night, and he sorted through them as if they were routine, vaguely aware of the ugly irony of that. Cabin fever ruined people, brought out the worst in them, and somehow it was always the children who suffered the most.

David rarely saw the actual events he reported. His domain was the aftermath of things. He worked on the assumption that he would always arrive after an event destroyed or dis-

abled whomever it was to destroy or disable, and he'd get the
facts while others swept up the broken glass or hosed away
the blood. He was usually dispatched from the newsroom by
Lemke, who sat beside the ever-squawking police scanner, listening with one ear while he carved away at the copy before
him. But there were also the chance occurrences when David
found himself in the middle of something. One summer evening he had stopped his car on the way back from a fishing
trip to see why several police cars were gathered at a cliff overlooking the river. Peering over the edge, he'd seen the body of
a man crumpled on a small wedge of sand one hundred feet
below. The man was dead, that much was clear, and David
didn't hesitate. He got a note pad from the glove compartment,
a stub of a pencil from between the seats, and approached the
four police officers gathered at their cars to await the boat that
would retrieve the body. In the back of one squad car a young
woman sat leaning into the seat as though her whole body
were numb. David got as close as he could, trying to pick out
the conversation between her and one of the officers. She was
trying to explain why she had sat on the rocks above for an
hour before going for help.

David preferred to arrive late at things. He found it vaguely
comforting. He never had to watch, only to talk to those who
had, to observe their mingled pain and horror, to coax information out from behind the noise of their shock and confusion. He
was skilled at it. But today had been different. His skills had deserted him because this time, he was a witness and he couldn't
surface from his own shock into the clearer air of the aftermath.

                              * * *

A long row of windows made up one wall of the newspaper office. That afternoon the room had been a blur of activity, as it

usually was before early deadline, but everything came to an abrupt halt when the voice of the front desk receptionist, returning from the break room downstairs, pierced the cacophony of phones, printers, and overlapping conversations.

"What's he doing?" she shrieked. "What's he doing?" First one person and then another abandoned their tasks and followed her gaze out through the windows to where a boy dressed in a light blue coat was creeping on all fours across the river ice, followed closely by his dog. He had a long stick and was tapping on the ice as he went. They saw him, but nobody could do a thing to stop him. Nobody had time.

Several people got up and ran to the windows. David moved as if by instinct, but now, in the warmth and comfort of his apartment, he felt shame to recall that his instinct was not to run outside and save the boy but rather to grab the notebook from off his desk. His first thought was that he was finally watching an accident, a news story as it occurred. The boy went farther out, then still farther, and someone, forgetting that the child could not hear him, shouted a warning. That had brought David back from his reverie and with a shudder he got up and ran for the door, hoping he could make it to the boy before the ice gave way.

He hadn't gotten far, not even past the last in the long row of office windows. His gaze was fixed on the boy and he saw the ice jolt and begin to give way. The boy, his balance shifting awkwardly, cast a look over his shoulder, a look that washed over David with its raw fear. Then the ice collapsed neatly, as if cut from beneath with a sharp blade, and the boy disappeared.

David was the first person to reach the river. He ran down the snow-packed embankment, his dress shoes sliding as he tried to pull up short at the river's edge. There was no sign of the boy. Even if he had been visible, grasping at the rough lip of the hole in the ice, David could think of no way he might rescue him. The exposed rim showed the ice was too thin for a full-grown man to traverse.

David felt a strange, placid feeling in the air, as though his ears were packed with cotton, as though the wind had ceased to blow and all traffic had stopped on the bridge above. Standing there, staring at the black opening where the boy had been crawling moments before, he noticed the lighted bank display across the river blinking over and over: *16°, 3:15.* Then there were sounds behind him—other people from the newspaper office sliding down the embankment, someone calling to him. Two squad cars arrived from opposite directions, skidding across the snow as they came to a halt near the bank. A young officer he didn't know emerged from one car and from the other came Janet Blake, the only female officer in the local force. She took charge quickly, sliding down the embankment and shouting as she approached David, asking what he had seen. He told her and they wasted no time laying themselves out on the ice in a human chain. One of the pressmen from the paper, a quiet old man named Rennett, had also joined them. Officer Blake, the lightest of the four, finally reached the hole and plunged her free arm in up to her shoulder. She groped furiously until she could no longer stand the cold and rolled back from the brink, her face a mask of pain.

In his mad dash outside, David had taken no coat with him and within minutes he was chilled to the bone. Reluctantly, he returned to the newsroom, but once inside, he realized he did not want to go back to the scene. He went to the bathroom, staying as long as he could, and emerged again, heading quietly to his desk, swiveling his chair so he sat with his back to the windows. He tapped at the keyboard occasionally, adding nonsense to the story he'd been working on before. That was when Lemke, the city editor, had descended on him.

"What do you think you're doing?" he asked David. Lemke's shirts were always wrinkled and he smelled bad, as though he used the bitter office coffee for aftershave. He smoked heavily, too, and David could smell the stale odors as Lemke leaned over his shoulder to peruse the screen. "I thought I saw you down at the scene there. That's your story, you know. You're supposed to be down there right now."

"No, that's not my story," David said abruptly.

"It damn well is yours, so you better get your coat and get back down there." Lemke had come around the front of David's desk now, resting his coffee cup on top of the computer monitor. David didn't look up.

"I've got one I'm working on," David said. "It's the one-car rollover on East Canyon Road. Besides, I still have the morning police reports to check downtown. I can't get to it. Vacarro's down there. Let him have it. He's taking notes like a madman."

"Well you go down there and ask for his notes, then. I want you to cover this." David didn't reply. Lemke's sour breath enveloped him, and he knew the man wasn't going to give it up.

"Look, I'm not asking you," Lemke said. "Don't give me any shit about this. That's your story, not Vacarro's. He's supposed to be at the city council meeting in a half-hour."

At that moment, David thought of standing up, taking his coat, and walking outside, not toward the river but toward the ratty bar across the street that he always avoided—that everyone avoided, except the pressmen who had claimed it as theirs. It would be dark inside, and quiet, and he'd order a stiff drink, something that burned going down. From there he could watch the whole thing transpire and never have to ask a question of another anguished parent or friend of the victim.

Lemke could fall through the ice, too, for all he cared. Maybe I ought to escort him out to the hole myself, he thought, and imagined taking the diminutive Lemke by the scruff of the neck, like a mewling kitten, and dropping him into the black.

"I'm waiting," Lemke said.

There was no use in resisting. He hated to admit it but Lemke was right. The boy, the hole in the ice, the red spin of the ambulance lights, these things were David's domain. "OK," David said. "Okay. I'll get Vacarro's notes." He rose, Lemke's eyes boring into the back of his head, and made for the door.

When he got down to the river again, little had changed except that there were more people. He found Vacarro interviewing two kids who said they knew the boy. He repeated what Lemke had said but Vacarro was reluctant to give up his notes.

"What's your problem anyway," Vacarro asked, his voice sharp. "Don't you get enough of this?"

"I get plenty. I didn't ask for this. Lemke said you're due at the city council meeting. He told me to get your notes." David waited while Vacarro tore several sheets from his pad and handed them to him. He knew they would be useless. Reporters write their own shorthand. It can't be shared.

"Did you get the kid's name?" he asked. Vacarro shrugged, a gesture that could have meant either no or get it yourself. Vacarro turned to go back up the slope. "Is there a positive ID yet?" David yelled, the frustration in his voice coming through. Vacarro was gone over the rise in the bank.

Experience told him he must find Blake. She would be considered the investigating officer. He tried a couple of cops until one directed him to the back of a paramedic's vehicle where she sat sipping from a cup of coffee and talking in hushed tones to the young officer who had arrived with her. She had exchanged her wet uniform shirt for a dry one and was wearing an oversized paramedic's jacket draped over her shoulders. Without his asking, she spoke.

"You already know all about this," she said the moment she saw David approach. Her voice betrayed her exhaustion, and the edginess David always encountered from cops who have tried, but failed, in a rescue.

"I know some of it, yes. But what about the boy—have you identified him?"

She frowned at him. "You know I can't give you that."

She was right and David knew it. But still, they'd been friendly enough on the occasions when their paths had crossed before. In one instance, at an arson scene that spring, she'd let him have access to the back of the supermarket that had burned down so he could survey the area investigators were examining as the likely source of the blaze. He wasn't sure why at the time—perhaps she hated arsonists more than other criminals and wanted a thorough news report. In any case, he had to try again to get inside the story of this boy who had fallen through the ice. He knew Lemke would ask, and he wanted to appease him with complete information.

"Look, I know you can't give me his name, officially I know you need a positive ID first. But what about off the record? I won't use your name as a source. I'll get independent confirmation." David waited for a moment and let the sounds of the rescue crews in the background fill the space. "I watched it happen, for Christ's sake." He wasn't sure why he said that, but it worked.

"It's unofficial," she said. "You didn't get it from me." He nodded, and Blake gave him the name of the boy she believed was the victim. She reminded him that until they found the body, it couldn't be confirmed. "On the record," she said, with a grim smile that pulled at the corner of her face, "I have no personal information about the accident victim to release at this time."

David thanked her and decided to look for the two boys Vacarro had been interviewing before. They were gone, so he began asking around to see if there was anyone else who knew the victim. He found a neighbor of the family who had come to the scene as soon as she heard a boy had drowned.

"I had a feeling," the neighbor said to David, shaking her head. "I had a feeling it was Timmy." She told David the boy used to rake her yard and sometimes he'd shovel her snow. "He was nine," she said, "only nine years old. A good boy. So young. I used to give him hot cocoa when he finished shoveling. He didn't say much, but he always thanked me. He was a good boy." As she talked, her eyes grew wet and then she began to weep, softly, quietly. David stood in the cold and dark, wanting to lead her away from the edge of the river where she was standing. Finally, all she could do was say the boy's name over and over.

The parents arrived at almost the same time, each having rushed to the scene from work. David overheard another person talking, explaining that the boy's parents were separated. The mother sat in stony silence in the back of a squad car. Occasionally her husband would come over, take her hand, talk to her, but David could tell she wasn't hearing what he said. The father finally became agitated. He was trying to convince the police to keep breaking up the ice downstream, to continue looking in the mounting dark for his son. He had begun to pace the bank, now and then unleashing a tirade at the nearest police officer, his arms waving and tears streaming down his face. They finally had to make him sit down in the back of a patrol car, not the one his wife occupied, and drink a cup of coffee.

David ran out of questions. He knew he ought to try to find the story of the people involved, the human interest angle as Lemke called it. People were loathe to admit it, but they were usually interested in learning specifically what had been snuffed out by death and he had proved good enough at finding it in the past. So many times, arriving at the scene of a disaster, in the rush of police lights, emergency vehicles, stunned and gawking people, he had let his own adrenaline take over. He was expert at discerning the difference between a mere passerby stopping for a look and a family member or friend of the victim or the perpetrator.

But this time, seeing the boy go under had changed everything.

The crowd eventually thinned out as dark came on. The clock read 5:15 and David slowly mounted the bank, his feet badly chilled, and headed for the back door to the office. The newsroom had emptied out as well, the day-shift people having gone home, replaced by a skeleton crew of editors and others whose job it was to stay late, sift through the raw material left behind by reporters, and put the day's issue together. He sat for a long time, the cursor on his monitor blinking, a loose assortment of notes and half-sentences straggling across the screen. Nothing was coming. He could feel Lemke watching him from across the room. The first draft he wrote was spare—Lemke took one look at it and scoffed at him.

"Could you try again? This has nothing—it reads like a goddamn police report." Lemke rolled his eyes, cleared the draft of the story from his computer screen. "Look, people were torn up over this. I saw the ad composers blubbering over their light tables downstairs. I mean, they didn't even know the kid. Don't you think you could put a little flavor into this?"

"Lemke, the kid drowned in a frozen river," David said. The

blood rose and pounded in his ears. "What flavor is it you're thinking of?"

"C'mon David, you're no pup. You know exactly what I mean. People are going to get up tomorrow morning and want to read about this. It's your job to make it interesting. They want to know more than the fact that he fell through the god-damn ice. Hell, half the town was down there anyway this afternoon. We've got to tell them what they don't know—like did you happen to find out why he was crawling out there on the ice in the first place?"

It was a ridiculous question. David felt the tiredness flooding through him.

"No, I have no idea. Nobody does. I suppose that really matters, does it?"

"Of course it matters." Lemke took a gulp of coffee. His cheeks bulged as he swallowed and stared at David.

* * *

An hour had passed after that conversation and he had still gotten nowhere. Deadline was closing in and David realized he had to do something. Lemke would use this against him somehow. He hardly cared about that, except that there was a hole in the paper waiting for his copy. David understood what that meant, but he kept seeing the boy's face, and then the father, pacing along the icy bank, the mother catatonic in the back of the police car. They would read the story, too, he thought. Or maybe not.

Not knowing what else do to, he took his coat from the back of his chair and put it on. Ignoring the stares of Lemke, he crossed the newsroom and went out the back door, going once more down to the river.

It had gotten even colder since the afternoon. The red neon

of the bank sign now read 8°. He saw lights glinting off a fresh skin of ice just forming at the edges of the hole. The snow was trampled thoroughly in every direction, pressed down by the crowd that had come to the scene. Then he heard a sound, faint at first, growing more distinct—a faint jingling from the far side of the river. He peered through the darkness until a shape emerged from the shadows and moved toward him across the ice. It was the boy's dog.

The dog approached the hole, slowing as it neared the place, crouching at the edge, muscles tense, ready to bolt. After a few moments it looked up at David, and then back to the ice. There was a long pause and for an instant, David thought the dog might lie down there, but then it turned to the opposite bank from which it had come and trotted across the ice for the shadows again.

The Sadness of Sister Maude

In the first scene of this story, you are in a shabby classroom. The air is still and hot on a late spring afternoon in the nether lands of rural New York state, the mugginess hinting of high summer to come. Your eyes move around the confines of the room, with its sullen ochre paint and windows open a slight inch or so to admit a thin stream of stale air, but you feel no movement at all. Just like you, the other kids sit limp and sweaty, fatigued. Even Theresa Murphy—the girl you have stared at now for two years, whose just-detectable breasts rise under her blouse like the holy mounds of a juvenile Mary— even Theresa Murphy looks melted, her shiny face propped upon her palm and a single bead of sweat forming just along her temple.

You hear the custodian, Mr. Burke, starting up the lumbering red lawn mower outside on the south lawn, a sound so distant it seems to travel from deep under an ocean of warm water. That's when you realize it has grown unusually quiet in the room. It isn't supposed to be quiet. Someone was reading aloud but now has stopped. You look up, orient yourself. She, the teacher, the woman at the front of the room, had been reading from a book, *The Last of the Mohicans*, a copy of which is propped open on your desk, on everyone's desk. You remember now and you look down to see your hand resting on the very page where the chapter ends, and when you remove your hand, dampness in the shape of your fingers puckers the cheap, pulpy paper. But she isn't reading any more. She has stopped. You don't know just when she stopped. You look up slowly, hoping her pale eyes aren't looking at you, eyes you think sometimes delicate and pretty, though you would never say such a thing or even think it too loudly, but you hope they aren't fixed on you, not because they would be angry but because they are always so sad and she is too young to have such eyes. You know this, even though this is only seventh grade and you are not old enough to fully understand the pure loneliness of a grown woman.

You look up but she is not looking at you. You see her face in profile, the strong angular jaw, square but not in a masculine way, the bones appropriately narrow and fitted to her slender neck. Her nose is prominent, but again, not so much that it seems poorly matched to her face. There is a wisp of her hair, a bright red-brown that you saw once in a magazine photo of Irish girls laughing on a street corner near the entrance to a convent school. She has that same hair, just a few strands peeking out from the tight rim of the white and black habit she always wears. You see again that she has high cheekbones, more clearly defined in the yellow light shining into the room from the high windows, light that falls just so on her face. Her taut expression gives way to a barely perceptible trembling, as if she will soon breathe out a sigh, or else cry out. But she does neither. Instead, she turns and surveys the class, her glance moving over you but not lingering.

Then Sister Maude does something you could never have

anticipated. It catches you, all the students in the classroom, by surprise. Even the boys whispering in the back of the room stop and the drone of the distant mower seems to pause at the edge of hearing. You see, everybody sees, that a tear has coursed down her cheek, and you swear you can hear it fall on the open page where her hand rests.

You check the book in front of you. It must be the passage she was reading. You feel that you should find that passage, that if you do, and if you read it, that maybe then she'll stop, that she won't be inside the passage any longer, that she'll stop crying. The emotion is too raw for you now, too close. You quickly read down, down, even turn the page, but there is nothing you recognize that could trigger this, though if it were years later, and you were a grown man, you would know. You wouldn't be looking in the book at all but out the window, toward nothing, and you would understand. When you look up, Sister Maude has risen from the front edge of the desk where she had perched herself to read. She straightens her simple black skirt as she moves again behind the desk and faces the chalkboard, composes herself briefly before speaking.

* * *

In the next scene of this story, you are in your bedroom. It is several weeks later, high summer. School is out. It's evening and crickets in the grass outside your window grow more bold and noisy as the light fades and you lie there thinking, curiously at this very moment, of Sister Maude. You imagine her lying in her own room, a spare, simply furnished chamber high in the northeast corner of the convent. You know the room to be hers because once you saw her at the window, when you were riding your bike at dusk and she appeared there, just a moment before she pulled the shade down. You thought she paused, though it was just a moment, to appreciate the breeze and the exchange of an orange sun for the cool, welcome canopy of the night. She did not have her habit on and you could see her hair, close-cropped but vivid, more red than you had guessed from the glimpses of strands that occasionally came free. She looked like any woman might as she stood by the window, like a young wife in her new home or an older sibling returned from college, changed, and you felt you should look away, as if she were naked before you, with her slender body and fair skin, with her eyes looking far away past the buckling pavement of the church parking lot, not even noticing you. Then she pulled the shade down and was gone and you kept riding, aware it was only an instant but more aware than ever because of seeing for once that her face was beautiful with her auburn hair framing it and not tucked away, out of sight.

Now, in your room, you imagine her life in the convent, a life connected by gravel paths between her cloistered cell and the high-ceilinged church and the muggy classroom where you know her best. You imagine her moving down the stairs of the convent, through the main lobby where once you stood that time you delivered the box of cleaning supplies from Mr. Burke. You see her walk out that door and across the blacktop of the playground, through the double doors of the school and up to the classroom, then back out the doors and again across the lot, but this time to the adjoining church with its great oak front doors, the ones they say are always open, then down the hushed aisle to the pew in the front, off to the right where all the sisters kneel together, their black habits bent in a row as all nine of them, even ancient Sister Claire, kneel and pray every morning. That would be it. Those would be the main paths of her life. There might be others, but you doubt they go far. You try to get inside her life, to imagine living it.

There is no reference point. You realize this. No one has ever thought to ask what the Sisters of St. Joseph do—are allowed to do—in their free time, in the evenings when you are gathered around a TV with your family or off riding around the neighborhood hoping to coax an extra half hour of light from the horizon where the sun has hidden. What do the sisters do? And as you lie there, trying to imagine shadowing her, and you hear neighborhood kids playing noisily in the street and the crickets growing louder, their scratching in unison as it always is, the time passes very slowly.

* * *

In the next scene you are in your room on a Sunday morning, approaching noon. The air is already thick with humidity and you are tying your tie before the mirror, making the knot as your father has shown you, hand over hand, through the loop, tighten. A sticky film already covers your body and you know the church will be like a greenhouse, dense and close, and that you will want to nod off when Monsignor Callaway mounts the pulpit to deliver another of his meandering sermons in a slurred language you barely recognize as English.

Your mother's voice reverberates from downstairs. Thomas, are you ready? Your father's ready to go. Let's not keep him waiting.

You pull your maroon sports coat from its hanger and reluctantly slip into it as you hurry down the stairs and out the door, which your mother holds open for you. A fine coat of powder on her face makes her look ghostly, but you notice already the beads of sweat on her brow.

Your father stands by the fender of your Ford station wagon, wood-paneled and rusting along the undercarriage from road salt and grime. He has rolled down the windows to let the hot

air escape, but as soon as you take your seat in back you realize it has made little difference. The car starts and your father
backs it out of the driveway, then turns toward the top of the
street.

It's hot enough to cook a Thanksgiving turkey in here, your
father says, loosening his tie slightly.

Rick, maybe we could stop for a cool drink after Mass, your
mother says. It might do us all some good, and it would be
something to look forward to.

I guess we could do that. Tom, are you interested.

You nod your assent, trying to seem enthusiastic, but the
heat is making you woozy and you're on the passenger side, in
the direct sun, which doesn't help.

Rick, do you remember, we're meeting the new priest today?

I wasn't aware they were bringing in a new priest, your father says, looking askance at your mother.

Well of course, they had to replace Father Schuyler, you
know.

Your father frowns, then looks over at your mother. I didn't
think they would be so quick about it, he says. What, he's only
been gone a few weeks.

Their conversation goes on like this for several minutes and
you listen as your mother informs him it's a young priest, that's
what she's heard from Rita Miceli, that he's come from a parish near Boston. You look out the window of the car at the lush
green leaves of the maples that line Curtis Street, at the sturdy
brick houses. This is the oldest part of town, close to the street
that runs along the wall of the penitentiary, the historic old
prison that was the site of the first execution by electric chair.
When you were in third grade, the classroom windows looked
out over the south lawn and you could see a corner of the high

wall, the green-glass turret at the top. You remember watching the guard, who would sometimes come out on the ledge for a cigarette. You would watch him smoke and lean over the rail, looking down at the courtyard where prisoners were shooting baskets or playing a game of softball. He was a prisoner, in a sense, just like the men he guarded, and just like Sister Maude.

You are surprised to find the inside of the church much cooler than you expected. It's a welcome relief, and you take your place in the pew alongside your mother, on the left side near the door where you always sit, at the foot of the statue of the Virgin Mary, who holds her hand to her breast and in her hand is a bleeding heart. She wears a pale blue hooded cloak over a white, full-length robe, her expression so profoundly sorrowful that sometimes you cannot take your eyes from her face. It has been this way for years, you there in your seat, or on your knees, at the foot of this image that is nothing more than a carving but still it captivates you. The words of the priests have long since ceased to mean much to you, but you come now to see Mary, to stare up and search for an insight to the melancholy smile barely perceptible in her expression.

The Mass begins. You move by rote through the standing, the sitting, the kneeling, the sitting again. The call and response is familiar and you mouth the words but give them no breath, wondering if this qualifies as praying—no breath, no spirit, no meaning. There are the readings from the Old Testament, then the New—this time one you recognize from the Book of John wherein Jesus interrupts the stoning of a prostitute, another Mary, and then gently pardons the woman when her would-be assailants—former customers?—have gone away. Go, and sin no more, he tells her. You look up at his mother; her expression has not changed. Does she approve? You assume she does.

The reading is over. Monsignor Callaway climbs the spiral stairs to the narrow pulpit, his girth nearly too much to fit inside, and you hunker down in the pew, resolved this time not to doze lest your mother pinch you fiercely on the thigh as she has done before.

Monsignor Callaway begins. Today I have the pleasure of introducing to you a new member of our parish community, Father Kenneth LaCroix. He comes to us from The Church of the Immaculate Conception in West Peabody, Massachusetts. Father LaCroix will be hearing confession this evening during regular hours, and I encourage all of you to stop by the parish hall for refreshments after the service so you can have a chance to meet him.

Monsignor Callaway turns and descends the steps of the pulpit and from the side altar you see the new priest striding toward the front. Although he has been there the whole time, you had not noticed him. He is a short man, and very young, perhaps no older than your Uncle Ted who is now in Vietnam and who sends you letters every so often with pictures of him next to his helicopter. But the most remarkable thing about this new priest is not his height or his youth but rather his long, brown hair, that flows down over his collar in waves. You glance up at the statue of Mary—still that enigmatic face—and you imagine that this is how her own son looked once, before the soldiers and politicians and peasants got their hands on him. His face is angular, his chin strong and square, and his eyes are lively. As he gains the top of the pulpit you want to applaud—why doesn't anyone applaud—but then you remember this is church, not a school assembly. He pauses a moment to look out over the assembled flock, his smile unmistakable and clear, not at all like Mary's, and then he begins.

* * *

In the next scene of this story, you are on a school bus. It is early October and the morning air, crisp and lovely, pours through the open window of the bus. The kids around you are wearing light jackets, their faces still sleepy and their voices subdued. This is a field trip. The teachers call it Conservation Day. You are heading for a farm and woods not far from the lake that dips its southern tip into the residential neighborhoods of your town, which is surrounded by thick-forested, rolling hills broken occasionally by a farm or orchard or vineyard. You like Conservation Day—you've always liked it and this will be your last because you are an eighth grader and will move on to high school next year, a place you've been warned is all about seriousness and rigor. You will be driving thirty-five miles to a prep school next year, an all-male academy where your father went and where you have known you would go since you first entered school. Since this is your last Conservation Day, you look forward to sneaking away from the crowd of students as soon as you can and heading for the secret trails you discovered on your visit two years ago, trails that lead to the waterfall where you can roll up the cuffs of your pant legs and wade across the edge of the spillway on the crumbling shelves of shale.

Sister Maude sits in the front seat of the bus, just across from Father LaCroix. They are chaperones for the eighth graders this year. You can see only the back of their heads, hers in the ever present black habit and his, the long brown hair ruffling in the breeze. Then she turns to speak to him and you see something you have not seen before—she is smiling broadly and her face is animated. She laughs, and you see how bright her eyes are, and that they are blue, which you have never noticed before. The priest laughs too, and suddenly you want to know what it is she said. Maybe you could remember it, remind her of it the next time you see her in class looking out the window, her face turned down to hide the thing inside that she cannot express.

When the buses unload at the side of the enormous old dairy barn, the kids spill out and immediately the chatter begins. It rises to a crescendo, with a few squeals and shouts thrown in, and two boys begin scuffling in the dust, playful but with an intensity that could only happen on a day such as this when the cool air of autumn signals the change of season. Father LaCroix steps into the center of the group of children and they circle about him. He raises his arms in the air, a toothy grin on his face, and the children grow quiet without his even having to say a word. Even the scuffling boys cease their entanglement and adjust their jackets and smooth down their hair, stepping to the edge of the circle.

I know you kids are excited, he says. I am, too. So let's not hold it in. On the count of three, let's all give a great big shout for Conservation Day. Are you ready? Okay, one, two, three. . . .

A great cry goes up from the assembled children, and you shout with them, a whoop that comes from the soles of your feet and rushes up the length of your frame. Father LaCroix laughs aloud and you hear it ring above the voices of the kids, and you hear another laugh, too. It's Sister Maude. Then you notice what you did not see before. She is not wearing her usual dress. She has on a short-sleeve blouse and a mid-length skirt that comes just to the top of her knees. The colors are still black and white but the effect is remarkable. And her habit is gone. The rich October sun splashes over her uncovered head, bringing out the copper highlights.

She stands next to Father LaCroix. The children hop up and

down, the girls grasping at one another's arms, the boys butting shoulders and tousling for position. You are standing back from the group a bit and you want to reach out and grasp the moment and capture it, freeze it, keep it forever. Instead, while the distraction lasts, you slip quietly toward the edge of the old barn and then behind it, casting one last look at the scene, and then you're off in a dead run for the copse of apple trees just beyond, the gateway to the secret trails where you will spend your last visit to this place.

The day turns out to be everything you've hoped. You are able to maintain a safe distance between yourself and the touring group as they visit the dairy barn, the silage bins, the great steaming heaps of dung whose purpose the farmer takes pains to explain to the giggling children. At lunch you sneak back into the group so as to not miss out on the meal, then secret yourself away again when Sister Maude calls for the children to gather up their wrappers and cups and move in an orderly fashion to the garbage bags at the back of the bus.

Back in the woods you make for the waterfall. It's a place where the nearby stream is at its widest and most shallow, perhaps fifty feet across. The water moves slowly as it approaches the precipice, a tumbling cascade that froths over a series of steps. You know the water is never more than knee-deep along this stretch, and if you're careful you can walk across the ledge of the falls to the other side. You take off your sneakers—this is the only day you're allowed to wear them to school—and plunge your feet into the water. It's shocking at first but after a few moments your feet adjust and you start across. Midway you stop and look around. The forest is a riot of color—deep yellow and orange and pale green, dark reds in the maples, and all the trees shedding leaves as if the letting go were orchestrated. Some fall and are blown out across the water, where they drop to the surface and come lazily down the course, a painted fleet heading for the falls.

A branch snaps in the woods and you stop moving. Through the dappled shade you see them—Sister Maude and Father LaCroix. Apparently, you are not the only one who knows of these trails. The two of them, still unaware of your presence at the crest of the falls, are walking along and talking no more than a hundred feet from where you stand. You can tell that if you go back the way you've come, you'll be visible to them in a matter of seconds and that the only way to go is forward, to hide along the bank beneath the footpath, so you dash quickly across the shale, the splashing of the falls enough to hide the splash of your steps. You duck under thick foliage that arcs out from the bank and after a few moments they pass on the trail only a few feet above you. You hold your breath with difficulty and listen as the nun asks the priest if he has found the new parish to his liking. He answers yes, and then adds a comment you can't quite make out and there it is again—the sound of her laughter blending with the wind and the waterfall as if it were native to that place.

You know it is wrong, that to eavesdrop violates their privacy, doubly wrong in that this is a priest and a nun, but you cannot help yourself. You follow, keeping below the bank and making sure not to lose your footing on the slippery stones at water's edge. You cannot make out much of their conversation, only the feel of it, the sound of his voice melodious and soft, his laughter and then again, hers. You try to imagine this version of Sister Maude at the front of the classroom, and how everything would be different, how the books would be more interesting, how the marks on your exams would be written in a more fluid hand, how her hair would blaze, always, just beneath the black habit.

Up ahead, the stream narrows and is crossed by an aged
wooden bridge, little more than two tree trunks with simple planks nailed across. You stop and hunker down behind a
bushy outcrop, waiting to see if they will continue on the path
or try to cross. Father LaCriox appears on the bridge, walking tentatively, and midway across he stops, turns back, and
smiles, then beckons with his hands. You see his lips move,
and though you can't hear what he says, it's clear enough. A
moment later, Sister Maude appears. The sun is bright, shining in your eyes, so you can't see her face or his. They appear
as silhouettes on a thin causeway, he standing with his arms
outstretched, she walking slowly, cautiously, measuring each
step, tottering a little, looking up from her feet to glance into
his eyes. She gets closer, and closer still, and as she nears him
her hand goes out and he grasps it.

Time stops. The leaves stop in midair, the water ceases to
flow past your bare calves, the water-skimmers on the surface
of the quiet eddies stop their twitching and there is no sound
at all. As quickly as it happens, it's over. They are at the edge of
the bridge, then off and onto the trail at the far side. He holds
her hand until she has taken a few steps on solid ground, then
relinquishes it and they move off down the trail on the other
side of the stream. You, however, cannot move. Your feet are
fixed in the cool water, your hands clutching the weedy stems
at the bank. You watch them walk away. They grow distant
behind the bushes and finally they disappear from sight.

* * *

In the last scene of this story, you are once again in the classroom. It is a different classroom this time, but it might as well
be the same—the same view out the windows, the sound
again of Mr. Burke's lawn mower moving across the expan-

sive lawn, the same smudged chalkboard and sour smells of young teenagers in their cramped chairs, the same woman at the front of the room.

Sister Maude is wearing her habit, as she always does. She is standing at her desk, her face drawn, a film of perspiration visible on her upper lip and brow. It is early May, the weather has turned hot and damp again, and out the window you see bulging gray clouds gathering in the sky.

Father LaCroix is gone. You learned about his sudden departure from your parents, although they didn't know you were listening as they discussed it in the living room late one night. He left just after Easter, when he had said High Mass for the last time. Your father told your mother it was for the best, that enough parishioners had made their feelings known that Monsignor Callaway really had no choice.

Don't you see, Meredith, your father said, his voice growing more hushed. He wouldn't have been a good fit for these old fuddy-duddies anyway. He was too . . . modern. And that hair. If he would have just cut his hair.

Your mother's voice was clipped, sharp, and you heard in it something you don't often hear—a challenge to your father. That's about what I'd expect from this town, she said. People talk, more people talk, and the next thing you know, there's no separating the lies from the truth. It's tiresome, if you want to know what I think. People think the worst. They're always ready to think the worst.

Meredith. Come on now. You know how it is. The church is an old institution. It has rules.

Oh, I know it has rules. Too many damned rules.

You know they can't have their own clergy violating the rules.

How do you know what went on? Were you there? Your

mother's voice came sharp, higher in pitch.

There was a long pause, and then your father's voice grew even more hushed. You couldn't make out most of what he said except something about even the appearance of breaking such a taboo being too much for Monsignor Callaway to tolerate. Your mother got up, you heard her tight footsteps on the kitchen tile, and a cabinet opened. There was a clinking of glass. She returned to the living room but the conversation was over.

You wake from your reverie and remember where you are. It's two forty-five in the afternoon and every kid in the classroom is watching the clock. Only twenty-five minutes until the bell rings, the blessed bell, and then the rush for bookbags and out the door, across the blacktop, down the street toward home. Only you won't be joining in. You haven't, not for several weeks now. It's hard to explain. Suddenly leaving the classroom feels different. You like to linger a few moments after the other kids have gone, shuffling with your books, straightening the pencils in the tray atop the desk, pretending to be busy so you can cast a glance at her, measure her face, look for clues.

Now she stands rigidly at the front of the room. Is she crying again? You look closely and see that her eyes are dry, her face implacable, fixed under the hem of the habit. Her hand is resting on the page from which she was reading but the room has grown quiet again. She is staring out the window, staring as if her eyes had found some distant signal over the hills or across the lake, a sail or bird on some high current. Outside, Mr. Burke's lawn mower chokes, throttles high, and stops. There is no breeze.

February

He sometimes wondered, after she left, if she also had trouble falling asleep at night. For months afterwards, every time he lay down he was overwhelmed by the feeling that his bed had become unfamiliar. It was the same bed he'd had for many years, but now it felt strange, an expanse of dry ground, the mattress stiff as the ones in hotel rooms. When he had stayed in a hotel room for several days running, even that bed began to feel familiar. This was his bed—it had been theirs for so long—and as the nights accumulated he lay down only to feel each time like a visitor tossing on a stranger's berth.

Things had gotten so bad that some nights he avoided lying down for as long as he could. Tonight was a night like that. He watched TV late, long after anything interesting was on, and then turned it off and stared out the front window, waiting for fatigue to catch up with him. Nothing moved outside—it was early February, well after two a.m.—and he was once again staring out the front window. A light fog collected most densely under a nearby street lamp, which cast barely enough light to illuminate the crusty snow edging the street. The whole town was pressed down under the curious winter fog, but he felt it gather more heavily within the frame of his picture window.

He thought about that, and then other things. An hour passed this way. He decided, finally, to lie down, and he moved through the darkened house toward his room. As he undressed by the side of the bed, a chill crept over his arms and back. He rolled back the covers and slipped in on the side he knew as his. The sheets settled on his body like mist, and then, before they had even begun to warm with his heat, the thought came to him as it had in nights past that he was somehow lying in the wrong bed.

The expanse around him felt poorly balanced, as though the mattress were a wide raft that might tilt and capsize from his weight on one side. He slid his leg across until his toes found the opposite edge. Before, they would have found something else. They would have never reached the edge. This was going to take more getting used to. He wondered how long it would be before he stopped noticing the tilt, the empty space around him.

Months later, he would figure out how to overcome it. He would finally learn to enter the bed on the opposite side, where she had always slept, and there he would fall asleep almost easily. But that understanding came much later, after summer arrived and he began opening the window at night to allow a breeze inside. For now, sleep remained a thing he had to struggle toward. For now, he lay awake on the side of the bed where he had always slept and imagined her where she slept in her new home, fourteen floors from the ground.

She had moved into a high-rise apartment building on the edge of a sprawling park near the city center. The building was an oddly narrow shape, a pale domino standing on end. He could picture her inside her apartment because he'd actually helped her move in. It wasn't so much a magnanimous gesture of acceptance, an attempt to show he was okay and could part from her on good terms. It was just that she needed the help and he knew that. He was accustomed to helping her, and hadn't managed to stifle the impulse to do so once more. She didn't ask for the favor but when he offered, she accepted. When he saw the rooms in her new place, he knew she'd be comfortable there, once she got settled and bought the right furniture. For a moment, he'd even thought about helping her out with that, too. She would have to buy a couch for the living room, and he knew where to get good reupholstered furniture at a bargain price. But he stopped himself, didn't say anything about it. That part was over, too.

He had helped her move all the bigger pieces—the chest of drawers, the stereo cabinet, the kitchen table. It took half a dozen trips back and forth between the house and the apartment building to move everything she had. Finally, he found himself carrying the last heavy box out of the elevator and into her apartment. He put it down just inside the door. Even with the boxes scattered everywhere and odd pieces of furniture left where they had hurriedly placed them, the rooms looked empty, as only a new home can before anything is unpacked, affixed to walls, stowed or arranged. The late afternoon light was failing quickly and the only lamp she had was as yet unplugged, leaving the room dim. He stood inside the doorway for a moment in the awkward and growing silence.

He hadn't anticipated this moment. He should have, but he hadn't. And then she came over to him, the last time she would ever do so, and saying nothing, put her arms around his neck and pulled him close. She was small, and he bent naturally to her embrace as he had learned to do, feeling numb, smelling for the last time the delicate scent of her hair. He looked through the open door of the bedroom and noticed where she had placed a small mattress on the floor against the far wall. They had not carried it in—it was something she'd gotten elsewhere. He had offered their bed to her, but she had declined. No, she had said, you keep it. It was yours when I moved in. You keep it.

So it was each night, when he lay down on his tilting raft, he recalled the view of her bed barely visible through the open door. The image remained as sharp in his mind as the scent of her hair and the feeling of her small and beautiful body, one last time against his.

Dead Man's Pants

I don't have much money. It's not usually a problem. I find ways of getting around it. I think most folks do. Most folks who don't have much money, that is. I eat a lot of spaghetti, for example. It's cheap, it's easy, and I can eat as much of it as I want. I can really stuff myself and it doesn't cost me much. I have spaghetti just about every other night and I never get tired of it.

My favorite recipe is one my friend Frank taught me. Frank was this fellow I met—he lived in the apartment above me for maybe nine or ten months and we never said more than hello to each other. Then one day he moved out and I didn't see him again for a maybe a year, until I ran in to him in line at the post office and we started talking. Then he invited me up for dinner at his new place, which was a tiny room on the top floor of an old house that he shared with a bunch of people. You could only get there by coming up this rickety old stairway in the back of the house. Frank sometimes had trouble with that because his hip was bad, but he never complained about it. I used to go over there all the time and we got to be pretty good friends. His window looked out over the railroad tracks that ran along the river, and many nights we sat talking, watching the trains pull in and then pull out again on their way west to Seattle or east toward Chicago.

Anyway, Frank had this favorite meal he used to make, which consisted of a loaf of garlic bread and a batch of garlic pasta—*olio* and *aglio* he called it—which was some version of a foreign phrase. He was Italian, so he knew about cooking, even on limited funds. He'd just grab two bulbs of garlic—and I mean bulbs, the whole head—and he'd whack them with the flat part of his big old butcher knife so he could peel and chop them up. He'd put some on the bread, with plenty of butter, and stick it in the oven, but he'd save most of the garlic for the noodles. He would boil those up in a bent up old aluminum pot. We'd drink some wine and when the noodles were ready he'd take about a half cup of olive oil, toss it in a hot skillet, and throw the garlic in with some salt and pepper. Then he'd just swoosh it around in the oil for a minute or two and dump the whole mess on the noodles, serving it up hot, with bread on the side and plenty of wine to go around.

That's the way I like my pasta, just like Frank made it.

Frank died in March, just when the weather was about to break. I remember that because it had been brutally cold for weeks on end and Frank had this awful cough that was acting up in the cold. He'd cough and cough, have these attacks, and sometimes there was blood and all that. I'm no doctor, that's for sure, but I knew he was in trouble. He wouldn't see a doctor. Besides, he was as broke as me. I think he knew what it was that he had, and that it wasn't going to get better. We were sitting in his room one night and he was really hurting bad. I had to make the food up and Frank just sat by the heater vent, wrapped up in an old wool blanket. He had dark circles under his eyes and the coughing—it made his whole skinny body rattle. After we'd eaten and had a bit of wine it seemed to relax him a bit, but he wasn't saying much and I was worried.

"Ed," he finally said to me, his voice hoarse from the coughing. "I believe my time is almost up." I didn't argue with him. I figure a man's got a right to speak the truth when he knows it and not have some fool try to talk him out of it. I poured him another glass of wine and we just sat and watched the trains.

"There are some things I wish I'd done," Frank said. "Things I should have done."

I didn't want to pry, and I figured he'd tell me what he meant if I just gave him a chance. But he didn't say anything else. I let it go at that, and I didn't bother giving him some speech about going to the doctor or checking into the hospital. I knew he'd never do it.

It was different for Ruth. She tried as hard as she could to get him to see a doctor.

Ruth was Frank's lady friend—I'd seen her visiting him many times when he lived above me, before we became friends. She's a small woman, kind of chunky and built low to the ground, but her eyes make her seem bigger than life. That and her hair—wild and bushy and silver with streaks of black left from when she was a younger woman. When she looks at you with her one brown eye and one green eye, hair flying around loose, you wouldn't say she's a beauty but you'd know you'd been looked at.

Ruth came around some nights when I was there and it was always a good time, the three of us together, drinking wine and laughing and telling stories. But when Frank got sick, Ruth had little patience for his putting her off about it. If he started coughing, and then explaining how he didn't expect to get better, she'd get downright angry about it.

"Frank, you old fool, stop talking like that before you talk

She nodded. "I was hoping you'd help," she said. But we both sat there at the table for a while longer and finished our coffee without saying anything.

When we did get up, I worked on the kitchen, putting knives and bowls and plates in a box that Ruth had brought for the purpose. Ruth started emptying drawers and pulling things from the closet. We didn't talk at all. Outside, the sun had come out and snow was melting along the edges of the street, leaving streaks of black where it trickled over the pavement. Ruth finished going through Frank's closet, pulling out the shirts and pants, the odd collection of beat-up shoes, a few dusty ties, a couple of old coats. She put it all on the bed. There wasn't much in the end.

Ruth turned to me. I knew what she was going to say a moment before she said it. "Why don't you take some of this?"

I shook my head. "I don't think I could do that, Ruth."

She wrinkled her face up and put her hands on her hips. "And why not? Frank don't need it any more. Besides, you're about the same size as him."

"I don't think so."

"Don't try to tell me you don't need it. I seen the way you dress. You're the raggedy man if I ever saw him." She reached down and picked up a pair of pants, in pretty good shape though there was a small hole near the back pocket where a button had been torn off. "Look at these—a perfectly fine pair of pants. Go on, take 'em." She thrust the pants out in my direction.

I looked into her face. I thought about trying to tell her I just didn't need any clothes, but that wasn't really true and we both knew it. I didn't want to argue with Ruth. I could see she was hurting as bad as me, maybe worse.

She put the pants on the bed and started moving deliberately about the room, her voice coming strong now, and I got the feeling that if she stopped busying herself for even a few moments that she might break down. We both felt it. So she kept picking up clothes, shaking them out, tossing them over to me, encouraging me to try them on. After a while, about half the stack was on my side of the bed. There was even a suit coat, in pretty nice shape. I'd never seen Frank wear it.

I kept quiet. In my head I started planning how if she made me take all that stuff, I could go past the homeless shelter on Center Street later on and drop it off in back. Now don't get me wrong, it's like I said—I could certainly use some new clothes. But there was just something about wearing a dead man's pants that made me feel uncomfortable, even if the clothes were better than what I had on and even if the dead man was my friend Frank. Maybe it was because he'd been my friend.

Ruth and I carried the things from Frank's closet down to her big old rusted out Oldsmobile. It was a pale green car, the vinyl top peeling like a week-old sunburn and the tires rubbed smooth all around. She had me put all the things I was supposed to take in the front seat between us and we drove off in the direction of the homeless shelter to drop off all the rest.

"Listen, Ruth," I said as we turned onto Center Street, "why don't we just give all Frank's stuff away. I'm sure there's some old guy needs it worse than I do."

She looked over at me with those wild eyes of hers and I knew I was going to get it. "Damn it, Ed, you just shut up about that. If Frank was here he'd tell you what I'm going to tell you. You just take these clothes and you wear them. They were good enough for him and they're good enough for you. There's plenty enough for other folks and no reason for you to give away things you need yourself. What's gotten into you, anyway?"

I stared out the window at the storefronts going by. "I'm just spooked about it, that's all."

"You're what?"

I was having trouble explaining myself. "I don't know. Putting them on . . . it would feel all wrong. They still belong to Frank. I haven't even really had time to think about him being dead."

She rolled her eyes and let out a sigh. We'd made it to the back of the shelter and she put the car in park and shut off the engine. "Listen. Frank is gone. Ain't nothing going to bring him back, and where he is, they don't wear pants."

I'd never thought of it that way but she had a point. She reached over and put her hand on my knee and gave it a little pat. "I know this is hard on you, Ed. It's hard on me, too. Frank didn't have but two friends in the world, and here we are. He ain't even been dead two whole days and we're sharing out the things he left behind. If he had a proper family, they'd take care of this, but I guess we're his family. So you go on and take some of those clothes that fit you. They'll last you a long while, and you can think of Frank and the good times you had together when you wear them. I know he considered you his best friend because he told me so."

Her comment caught me off guard. For the first time in years I felt tears coming to my eyes and I looked away, out the window of her car and across the lot. "I just don't know, Ruth. It's all kind of happening too fast."

"Aw, nonsense. Sure it's a shock right now but when Frank's been gone a while we'll be able to get past how we feel. Then you'll be glad to have his things around. If I'm wrong about that, then you can bring them on down here after all." She stopped and looked right at me, waiting for my response. "Is it a deal?"

I nodded.

We got out and unloaded the things we were giving away. This skinny kid with bad skin stood at the door to the shelter smoking a cigarette and watching us, but he didn't help unload. When we were done, Ruth drove me over to my place and she helped me carry the rest of the things in and hang them up. I felt better after seeing them in my closet. We went back to Frank's place and got another load of stuff, the last of it. Ruth also made me take Frank's lamp, a few pots and pans, and the dented softball bat Frank had always kept around. He said it was for defending himself, if the need ever arose. I didn't figure I'd ever have the need but I took it all the same.

When we were done unloading it all, I felt easier about things. "I guess you're right about how Frank would want us to have his things," I told Ruth, even though I wasn't entirely convinced. She was in the driver's seat and the sun was going down behind her so it shined through her hair and made a kind of halo around her face. "Frank would want us to use what we can, I'm sure of it. He would want us to think of him in the best ways," I said. "But I sure am going to miss him."

That's when she came over and gave me a hug. It wasn't any big deal, except that it had been so long since a woman had done that, I had almost forgotten what it felt like.

* * *

It took me a while to get used to the idea of Frank being gone. Sometimes I'd wake up and the first thing I'd think of was walking over to Frank's to watch a bit of TV on his broken-down set with the sound that used to cut in and out. A couple of times, out of habit, I'd wake up and start getting dressed to go to Frank's, but then I'd open the closet and there they were, his shirts hanging up on the far side. Just like that I'd remember, and then I'd feel like a fool.

I didn't wear his things. I couldn't. I just let them be. Eventually I stopped worrying about it so much.

By May, spring was coming on hard and fast. I found myself thinking more of the good times I'd had with Frank, just like Ruth had said I would. So one day when I went to my closet to dress, I saw his clothes and I decided to put some of them on. I put on Frank's gray wool pants, the nicest ones he'd had, and one of his flannel shirts. It was a bit tight in the shoulders but not too bad. Then I walked downtown for a cup of coffee. The clothes felt all right, and nobody noticed that I was wearing dead man's pants, or if they did, they didn't say a word.

A few days later I got up the nerve to start wearing some of his socks, which was a little strange. I mean, there's something about socks. You don't usually think of them, but there I was, walking down the sidewalk aware of every step. But I liked having some fresh socks, as all my pairs had gotten so worn out they were more holes than cloth.

Finally, I worked my way up to the thought of wearing the suit jacket. It was a nice one, and it's kind of funny that even though I'd never seen him wear it. When I put it on, I really found out who Frank was.

It all happened because of Ruth. We'd begun to get together now and again—the first time was a few weeks after Frank died when she came by and asked if I wanted to stop over to her place for some of that garlic pasta he used to make.

"So you're hooked on that, too?" I asked her.

"C'mon," she said, "it's about all we ever ate together. I think it's time we celebrate old Frank by cooking up a pot of those noodles in his honor." I joined her that night and she made it just like Frank used to. We had coffee after dinner, and some cherry pie she'd made. It was damn good. We talked late into the night, and though we couldn't see the trains from her window like you could at Frank's, we listened for the whistle until it came floating over the town. I'd say it was romantic, if that word didn't sound so funny when talking about a couple of shabby people like Ruth and me. I didn't think of us as a couple, but it was good to be with a friend. After all, we had that much in common: both of us had lost one and we felt the need.

We saw each other about once a week after that. I looked forward to it quite a lot. I should say that I never touched her, except sometimes a hug when I left. Sometimes she'd come over to my place, but since I don't clean up much around here it was always better to go over to her place.

One night, I guess it was about early September, she came over with good news—she'd gotten a new job as a swing shift clerk at a gas station a few blocks from my place.

"Let's celebrate!" she said. "Let's go out and eat."

"Well, we never have done that before," I said, "but if you're offering to treat me, I won't complain."

"Of course, it's on me. You go on and get cleaned up, and I'll be back in an hour to pick you up—got to run a couple of errands first."

I took a quick bath, brushed my hair, and went to the closet to get dressed. I decided to wear Frank's suit coat since I was going to dinner with a lady and it was only right to wear my best clothes. First I picked out the gray wool pants and a nice green shirt of his and put them on. I grabbed one of the ties, a grey one with silver diamond shapes all over it, and beat it against the closet door a few times to get the dust out. I'd forgotten how to tie one so it took me four or five tries to get a decent knot. Then I grabbed the coat. It was the first time I'd taken it out and tried it on. I slipped my arms into it, checked the fit in the mirror.

It felt a little tight around the middle and I couldn't button it, but it wasn't too bad. Then I put my hand in the pocket—the little breast pocket on the inside—and I found the package.

It wasn't really big enough to call it a package, just a thin bundle of brown paper with a string tied around it. I hadn't noticed it there when we'd first brought the coat over to my place. I sat down on my bed and tried to think what I ought to do. Open it up? Even a dead man deserves his privacy. I thought about tossing it in the trash, but that seemed even worse than opening it. I started to think it might be okay to open it. Frank was dead, so he had no privacy to protect anyway. "He's gone," I said aloud. "Maybe I was meant to find this."

I untied the string, folded back the paper, and found myself looking at a picture of a little boy. It was a black and white photo and it was old, the edges yellowed and worn. I couldn't say exactly how old, but I guessed maybe forty years or so from the way the boy was dressed in a pair of short pants and a button-down, long sleeve shirt. He was squatting by the back stairs of an old row house, hammering away at a small wooden box with a mallet. A breeze was blowing through his black hair. I turned the picture over and on the back, in a woman's handwriting, it said, "Jimmy, 3."

That was all. Just the boy's name and age. And I couldn't say why, but somehow I knew I was looking at a picture of Frank's son. Frank had never mentioned a thing about having children but looking at that picture, it all made sense. Somewhere along the line, back when he was a young man and before his life had fallen down, he had fathered a child. Where was this little boy now?

There were other things in the packet. There was a religious medal with a picture of the Virgin Mary on one side and on the other, a thorny crown wrapped around a heart. It was

held in a tiny leather pouch that somebody had sewn by hand.
There was also a letter. It was folded up and the paper felt brittle. I tried to be careful opening it but the envelope cracked
into two pieces. I removed the sheets from the halves of the
envelope and laid them out on the bed. The writing was badly faded—too faded for my eyes. I tried to read it but I couldn't
make out the words.

The last thing I found, rolled in a tight tube, were five one
hundred dollar bills. The rubber band was so old it broke into
fragments as soon as I pulled at it.

That's when Ruth arrived. I heard her knock and I called
out for her to let herself in. She came down the hall and turned
into the room, smiling and about to say something, but she
stopped herself short when she saw the things laid out on the
bed.

"Oh," was all she said, just like that, and her face went soft.
It was the first time I'd ever seen that look on her face, surprise and maybe just a little bit of confusion. I wasn't expecting it. She'd been so much in control of herself when Frank had
died and the whole time we were over at his place cleaning out
his closet and drawers, but now she stood speechless, her eyes
working over the items.

"These were in his coat pocket," I told her. "I just found
them a few minutes ago." Ruth nodded, and then came over
and sat down on the bed. One by one she picked the things up,
turned them over in her hands just like I'd done. She looked a
long time at the picture of the little boy, then she tried to read
the letter. There was no way. The writing was hardly more
than a suggestion, little wisps of smoke that couldn't be made
out. But I also knew Ruth was figuring it out the same as I had.
The letter and the photo were together, and it was a letter from
the boy's mother.

"What's that?" she said, pointing to the roll of bills.

"It's an awful lot of money, that's what it is."

A look of surprise crossed Ruth's face. "How much?"

"Five hundred dollars." You couldn't really tell, the way the bills were rolled up, so I tried to smooth one out on the bed but it sprang back to its tube shape. I watched Ruth, not sure what she would say, not sure what we ought to do.

"Frank never told me he had a kid," Ruth said, her voice slow and thick. "But I had my suspicions. There are just certain things about the way a man acts around kids and that will tell you whether he's the type to have any himself. We used to go down to the park on Cypress Street. You know the one by the elementary school. The kids would just run to Frank. He'd be covered with them, like they were bees. And he loved it, he sure did. He never said it, but that's why he liked walking to the park instead of down past the river. He'd tell the kids stories, tell them riddles. He'd ask their names. Once he lugged his old chessboard down there and taught some of them to play chess. These are kids who don't have nothing," Ruth said, shaking her head. "Some of them act like nobody's paid attention to them in years."

There was a long silence, and then I said what was on my mind. "So how do we find that boy and send this money to him?" I asked.

Ruth's voice was flat. "Have you got any idea how to find him?"

I had to admit, I didn't. I picked up one of the brittle squares of paper. I looked at the envelope for a return address but there wasn't any. There wasn't even a postmark. It must have been hand-delivered. I pictured it sitting on the breakfast table in a shaft of morning sun. Maybe that's where he found it.

Ruth squinted at the writing on the paper, held it up to the light, and then frowned. "That boy doesn't exist anymore. Not really. We'd have to look for a middle-aged man with only this old picture to work from. I'm no detective," Ruth said, "and from the looks of you, Ed, I guess you aren't either."

A moment later Ruth got a mischievous smile on her face, and then she stood up and put on her coat. "I got a plan. For most of this money. But first, what do you say we go out and get us that dinner? I don't think Frank would mind springing for it."

* * *

I don't eat in restaurants too often. Once and a while I go to the diner near my place for coffee and, when I'm holding a little cash, maybe a sandwich. The restaurant we went to was good, and the food was even better. The waitress was young and she spilled my glass of wine, but Ruth and I laughed, and then the girl did, too. At the end, Ruth cashed one of the hundreds and left the waitress a tip as big as the price of the dinner.

The park wasn't far off. We left Ruth's car in the restaurant parking lot and walked. The air was cool and the sun was slipping below the edge of a cloud front, casting a bright yellow light across everything. I worried that there might not be any kids in the park by the time we got there, but as we got nearer I heard their shouts and knew they hadn't gone home yet.

They were off in the distance and I could hear their voices but not what they were saying. We stopped by the playground and watched them for a while. They were playing football. Their clothes were muddy. One boy was playing barefoot, another had taken off his shirt, which lay in a wad by the base of the tree that must have marked one goal line.

I waited. I wasn't sure how Ruth was going to do this. There were eight of them, and she had only four bills. But look-

ing closer I saw that two of them had the same thick shock of
blond hair and they had to be brothers, and then I saw another likely pair, maybe even a third boy who must belong with
them, all with bright red hair and freckles. Ruth got up from
where we were sitting and started walking toward the group. I
stayed behind and watched her. At first they didn't see her, but
then one boy pointed and the others stopped what they were
doing. After a minute I realized they were looking for Frank.

Then they gathered around her. They stood listening to
her, several of them with their hands pulled up inside the loose,
muddy sleeves of their sweatshirts. The bare-chested boy held
his arms across his chest and seemed to squeeze himself. Ruth
kept talking. I couldn't hear what she said. And then she pulled
out the money. I saw her peel off the first bill and hand it to the
tallest boy. His two brothers moved closer, looked at the paper.
I knew they weren't used to seeing a $100 bill. She dispensed
the others, and then with her hand she pulled the smallest of
the children to her and held him for a moment.

Train Going Away

The room looked tiny—much smaller than I remembered it. That's what struck me as I stood in the glaring sun, hands cupped to the window so I could see through the filthy glass. Dust swirled in shafts of light, marking the emptiness. The woman and her little boy had gone, along with the ratty furniture they'd scrounged from alleys and the chipped plates and cups that were always piled high in the sink.

I knew the room wasn't any smaller than it had been. It was just the unexpected absence of her and the boy that had made my life suddenly shrink. I didn't quite understand it then. Now I know all too well how that works. I've had more practice at it.

I was nineteen and a stranger in Southern California. My brother had been kind enough to let me stay at his place while I tried to earn some money. I think he understood how it was to run out of options. I'd suffered through one aimless year of college, then bailed out and went off on my first big mistake—an ill-advised adventure in eastern Wyoming. A friend had lured me there on the promise that his survey crew had regular work. He'd exaggerated. All they offered was for me to fill in a couple days a week for guys who regularly drank themselves sick in the small town bars. The high plains nights were cool, the skies deep blue and awash with more stars than I had ever seen, but I was soon more desperate than I'd been when I arrived. I never had even a hundred dollars to my name that whole summer and after listening one August night to an old guy's story of a winter he'd spent in a drafty sheep trailer, I used all my cash for a hot meal, a phone call to my brother, and a bus ticket.

This story is not about any of that. It has more to do with a woman I met in California, and her four-year-old son. Her name was Carol. She had a thick New Jersey accent and an attitude to match. She was short, barely five feet tall, with olive skin and brown eyes, and she wore her wavy brown hair in a long ponytail. We met at the Parks and Recreation district office, in a line of ragged people looking for work. It was a long wait, and eventually we started talking. I told her about my friend and his miserable survey crew, and she said she'd been to Wyoming, too, a long time ago. She said she ended up in L.A. because that was where her ancient Chevy pickup truck finally broke down. She didn't exactly say where she was headed when it happened, or where she'd come from, and I didn't ask.

After filling out the applications we smoked cigarettes out on the patch of lawn in front of the office and then she said goodbye because she had to get back to her little boy who was home alone. I didn't expect to see her again. I'd also given up on a job with the city when a few days later I got a call that there was work mowing lawns at various parks.

The first day, when I showed up to work at the maintenance yard, I saw Carol. She was loading saplings onto a flatbed trailer when I arrived. She didn't miss a beat, as though our conversation a few days before had never really ended.

"I told them to hire you," she said with a grin. "I'm glad to see they took my advice."

"Thanks," I said. "You don't know how bad I needed this."

She gave a little laugh and shook her head. "Yes, I do," she said. "Yes, I do."

That day after work I offered to buy her a coffee. I wanted to show my appreciation. Little did I know it would get to be a habit. Soon we were going a couple times a week to a greasy spoon on Prairie Avenue, where we would share a large plate of French fries and drink a whole pot of coffee. She always stopped off at her apartment to pick up her little boy, a scruffy, quiet kid named Robbie. He had the same wavy hair and big, brown eyes, and I thought he was about the most easy-going kid I'd ever met. A lot of the time he was off in his own world, playing some kind of ongoing outer-space adventure with sugar packets and straw wrappers for spaceships. Occasionally he would look up at me and smile, then go back to his game. Sometimes I would float a French fry spaceship into his little universe, expecting him to shoot his lasers and blast me to bits, but he always just sidled up to my vessel and made friends with my spacemen. Robbie liked to have a vanilla milkshake with his fries. I guessed from the way he ate it was probably his main meal each day.

An endless capacity for hot coffee was a clue about Carol. I soon learned that Carol liked to speed and I became her passenger. She often brought along to the restaurant these little white pills. The first time she offered them, I didn't hesitate, afraid I'd look like a fool. I nonchalantly took several and chased them with a swallow of coffee.

Carol gave a little laugh and poured one into her palm. "I prefer to snort them," she said, and excused herself to go to the restroom. I hadn't expected that.

The next morning, my hands were still jittery. I hadn't slept at all.

Although I became her friend, we weren't lovers. That seems important to mention, though I'm not sure why. I just remember that I spent a lot of my free time that autumn with her and Robbie, and for the first time in a while, I was content. I had a bit of money from the lawn mowing job and could pay my brother for food and rent. He never asked for it, but I would put money on the kitchen table after payday and he accepted the gesture.

Sometimes after our "meals," Carol, Robbie, and I would walk across the tracks—I mean this literally—to her shabby apartment. We'd talk late into the night, listening to the radio and watching out the window as the occasional freight train would lumber past. We'd have a couple glasses of cheap wine if we had enough money, and more of the little white pills from her endless supply, and Robbie would play with his simple toys: plastic margarine tubs, a branch from a dead bush out front, and his favorite, a filthy, tattered stuffed animal. Carol would tell stories in her Jersey accent and when she laughed, I could see that laughing didn't chase the dark circles from under her eyes. But I liked it when she laughed, and I felt at ease there on the dirty carpet, where we sat for lack of any chairs. Even after I'd helped her to scrounge a couple of battered chairs from the alley nearby, we'd still sit on the carpet.

"You know," she told me one time, "I can't figure out why you hang around here. I mean, how old are you?"

"I'll be twenty soon," I said.

"Why aren't you out chasing down girls and getting your share of pussy, like most of the other guys your age?" As she said this, she blew a stream of cigarette smoke in my direction. I wasn't used to women talking like this, though it was common enough among guys. But Carol was different from any woman I'd ever known and that's what I liked about her.

I shrugged. "I don't like chasing," I said. "Besides, there's no hurry."

"Oh, there will be," she said. "But that still doesn't explain what you're doing here."

I realized she actually wanted some kind of honest answer. I looked around the room a moment, took another swig from the bottle of wine. "I guess I just like hanging around with Robbie. Great kid, you know."

She smiled, looked over at her son, then back at me. She was about to say something, but didn't.

* * *

My brother's place was in Carson. That's not one of the pampered beach cities. It's a gritty place inside the smog belt where the heavy, ochre air settles in on hot days, where the aging strip malls are interspersed with dense rows of shabby stucco dwellings, ringed by palm trees all slouched and grey with disease. Carol's neighborhood was tucked behind an industrial park that was still served by a rail spur, the kind of place where every ground level window has iron bars and where harried looking store owners pull accordion gates across the entrances to their graffiti-laced stores each evening.

We had been hanging around together for almost two months when I showed up unexpectedly one Saturday at her place. She opened the door, looking very tense, and waved me in, a cigarette in her hand. Robbie was sitting on the back porch steps—I could see him through the open screen door.

A man was leaning against the kitchen sink, his powerful arms and stained overalls suggesting he worked around heavy machinery. To my surprise, he nodded at me. I took a seat on a dilapidated couch, which hadn't been there before, the thought running through my head that I shouldn't be in that precise spot at that particular moment. Don't stay long, I told myself, just long enough to keep from looking like an idiot—but it was already too late for that.

Carol ignored me for the moment and went over to talk with this guy, their voices hushed, their words nothing I could make out. I wasn't really trying to hear them, and after it went on for a few moments, I got up and walked toward the door.

"Wait," Carol said, "don't leave."

I explained that I had just stopped in on my way home, which was a lie, and that I had to get going, which was also a lie because I had nowhere to go but back to my brother's apartment.

"Wait," she said again, this time more urgently. The man was still standing where he had been before, his arms crossed over his chest and his face expressionless. I told Carol I'd have a smoke out on the porch, and she tossed me the pack that was on the counter.

It just so happened that as I stepped outside, a freight train was coming from a short distance off and making its slow way down the center strip that ran the length of the street. I lit one of the cigarettes and watched the train's slow advance, then stepped out into the street and moved toward the tracks. The train finally crossed the spot a few yards away from where I stood and I found myself wondering what was in the dusty cars, screeching and lurching past.

Then, suddenly, there was somebody beside me.

It was the man from Carol's apartment. He nodded at me again—really just a jutting of the chin that some guys use as a greeting—and he indicated the cigarettes. I handed him the pack, he took one out, and then with a deft shake of his wrist set another cigarette protruding out of the pack. I figured I had better take it, and I did. He stowed the pack in the breast pocket of his overalls.

So there I was smoking, which I rarely did before meeting Carol, alongside a man I'd never met and about whom I knew little. A strange worry knotted in my gut, nothing I'd ever felt before. Then an even stranger thing happened.

"I'm Robbie's father," the man said above the rumble of the box cars. His voice was calm and matter-of-fact, and I thought I saw him smile as he said it. "I came round because tomorrow's his birthday. I try to come around on his birthday."

Now it was my turn to nod. I took a drag on my cigarette and tried to make myself look older, which was of no use. But he didn't show any contempt and I realized he hadn't come out to threaten me, as I had feared.

"You known Carol long?" he asked.

"Not really," I said. "A couple of months. I met her at work."

He nodded again, then said, "Robbie doesn't much like the fact that she's gone some days, but it's a good thing that she's found work."

"Robbie's a good kid," I said.

The man nodded. "He's a good kid," he said.

I don't know what made me say it, but the words escaped before I could rein them in. "I try to be nice to Robbie," I said.

It was true. A week earlier I had brought him an old baseball glove I'd found at my brother's house, though I didn't think far enough ahead to bring a ball. When I gave it to Robbie, he didn't know what it was. I had to put it on his hand, which looked so small in the mitt that I immediately felt stupid for bringing it. I got an orange from the counter and used it as a ball, showing him how to catch a short toss. He learned quickly and we only stopped when the orange split and started oozing. Carol couldn't hide her amusement.

I told the man about the baseball glove although I wasn't so sure I should.

"That's good," the man said. "He's old enough now he ought to learn to catch."

The pause filled the night air between us as we stood shoulder to shoulder, and without looking at the man, I said, "You know, I just think I ought to say about Carol and me, it's not what you might think."

The man took a long drag on his cigarette and shook his head slowly from side to side. "That's no matter to me," he said. "I got a woman of my own down in Long Beach, and a baby boy."

I nodded. I could see, down the track, the last car on the train. We both watched it grind slowly toward us. "I wonder what's in these train cars," I said as the last one reached the spot where we were standing.

He paused while it receded, shook his head again. "Nothing in those cars," he said. "That's how you know they're leaving."

We finished our cigarettes in silence. He nodded once more toward me, went to his car, a restored late sixties model Impala, and drove off along the avenue, the street lamps glowing orange overhead.

* * *

It wasn't long afterward when I arrived at work one morning and found the manager waiting to talk with me. He'd noticed that Carol and I often left work together and had probably assumed I'd know why she hadn't shown up at work the last couple of days.

"You have any idea where she is?" he asked. "She's got no telephone so I can't check up with her. Is she sick or something, or maybe the kid?"

"I don't know," I told him.

He looked at me a long moment. "If you happen to talk

with her, let her know I've got a list as long as doomsday of people that want the job and I won't hold it for her past Friday. You tell her that."

I decided I would check in on Carol after work. It was a long day. My jeans and sneakers were stained green and my ears were ringing from hours behind the mower. On my way to Carol's place I stopped at a liquor store where I knew the owner, a bent old man who was mostly deaf, would sell me a bottle of wine so long as I bought a sandwich, too. The store was just down the street from Carol's apartment. I remember thinking to myself as I crossed the train tracks that if I didn't know better, I would have guessed no train had ridden those rails in decades.

When I got to Carol's place, I knocked. No answer. I knocked again, louder this time, hoping she was just asleep.

I finally turned to go and saw the sun glint off the window where the ragged drapes had been slightly pulled back. I turned back and when I cupped my hands to the window and peered inside, I could see the place was empty.

Woodcutter

The rock came out of nowhere and hit Ethan so hard on the neck that he tumbled backward down the hill, his skin and clothes collecting twigs and moss and leaves along the way. When he finally stopped rolling and regained his feet, he stood unsteadily, spitting out bits of earth, a strange half-man, half-tree creature too dazed to know what had happened.

He knew he'd been struck by something—that much was clear from the welt rising on the flesh just below his ear. He put his palm to the place and it felt hot and raw. There was no blood. Ethan shook his head and brushed the bits of leaf and dirt from his hair.

Just then something moved in the brush beyond the place where he'd been squatting moments ago, chopping away at a smooth log. Was it a bird? Something larger? He squinted and peered into the dappled shade, his eyes scanning the madroña trees, hoping to pick up movement of whatever animal they concealed.

Then it dawned on him. An animal might mock charge, might recoil and hiss, might even attack with fangs and claws, but he could think of no animal that when threatened or hungry would throw a rock. Maybe certain primates would have the inclination and necessary opposable thumbs to manage the act, but there were no apes native to coastal California forests. Unless he'd been accidentally hit by a falling branch or something like it . . . but no, this had been a projectile, aimed at him, and for some reason he had the feeling it was aimed with enough skill to miss his skull—just barely—and strike where it would do no serious harm but would serve as a warning.

A branch snapped. Loudly. Ethan crouched low to the ground, his eyes again frantically scanning the patterns of brown and green dappled with yellow light cast by the late afternoon sun. He'd rolled far enough down the hill that he couldn't see the ledge above him now where he'd been wielding his axe. He had dropped the tool when he was struck. It was a brand new axe he'd bought just before coming on the trip, having anticipated that October camping, even on the coast, would necessitate a fire for warmth. His head was throbbing now and as he leaned into the hillside he thought to himself, I've got to get that axe. I'm not leaving it behind.

Ethan began to climb slowly up the hill on all fours, his hands ready to defend against whatever might come hurtling out of the bushes. He was alert for any sign of movement. Wind surged lightly through the leaves of the madroña trees and beneath that, the river's cascade sang a descant. His movements slowed even more as he crested the hill.

A man was sitting on the log Ethan had chopped, his hands playing over the few shallow nicks in the wood Ethan had managed to make before being dispatched. He was bare except for a dirty cloth around his waist. His skin was a warm, brown color and Ethan mistook him as Mexican until he noticed his hair—dark, yes, but from dirt rather than natural color. Fair-colored wisps of hair flew away in all directions from

the tangled mass on his head, and his eyes were a pale green
shade, not far off the color of the river below. He wasn't large;
in fact, he was smaller than Ethan and skinny, although in a
tough, wiry way.

Ethan's axe, its bright yellow handle contrasting with everything else in the scene, lay in the dirt at the man's bare feet.

The man's hands continued to caress the log as though they
might heal the notches and smooth the wood back to its orig-
inal condition. The hands themselves belied the man's age.
They were too large for his small frame, rough-skinned, the
knuckles crossed with scars. Ethan looked more closely at the
man, whose face was still focused on the task before him. He
must be about fifty years old, he thought. Maybe more.

As he watched from his crouch, Ethan tried to think what
he should do next. The welt on his neck ached, reminding him
that whatever else he did, he should not forget that this man
was hardly some benign forest sprite. He felt a cramp in his
thigh and shifted a bit to alleviate it, rustling some leaves in
the process.

The man raised his head, slowly. His eyes were at first wide
open and empty but as he met Ethan's gaze, they narrowed
and hardened. Ethan froze. He fought an impulse to charge at
the man, knock him from the log, seize the axe, and make a
run for it.

The sound that came from the man's throat was primal—a
shout, but also a shriek of outrage and pain. It was much like
the sound that had come from Ethan when the rock hit him,
but this man's voice didn't form any known word. It was just
a cry, shapeless but expressive nonetheless. He glowered at
Ethan for a moment, grunted softly, and without looking away,
reached out and grasped the axe.

This is not happening, Ethan told himself. You're having an

hallucination. You're back in camp, sleeping off the long day's hike. But he didn't believe that—his tender neck proved he was awake—and there was nothing he could do but wait for the strange man to make his move. Ethan calculated the distance to the bottom of the hill, where there was better cover. He could make it in a matter of seconds, and surely his boots would allow him to move more rapidly over the rough terrain than would the man's bare feet. Or would they?

The man let out another cry, this one less angry than the last. Was it a question? It sounded like one, rising in tone at the end. Sweat beaded on Ethan's brow and rolled down into his eye, stinging. He dared not wipe his face lest any quick movement spook his adversary. His neck hurt enough from the rock; he didn't want to think of what the man could do with a hand axe still factory sharp.

The man raised the axe and brought it down with alarming force on the surface of an exposed boulder. Sparks flew and the ringing of metal on stone drove birds from the trees all around them. Ethan crouched lower and made ready to bolt, but held his ground a moment longer, still unwilling to abandon the tool and not convinced fleeing would be the wisest move anyway. Another stroke, more sparks and music, then another and another. Even from where he squatted twenty feet away, Ethan could see the new blade was badly notched from its contact with the stone.

The man's fury rose for a few moments, subsiding only after the blade had been dulled along its entire length. He let the axe slide from his hand back to the ground and then he stood up. He was no taller than a young teenage boy but Ethan saw again the strength in the hands and sinewy limbs. The man picked up the far end of the log, which was about as thick as his calf, and dragged the whole thing off into the bushes.

There was much snapping of twigs and rustling, and then the strangest sound yet: weeping, soft and pained. Ethan heard it clearly. It faded away slowly and then, the forest was silent again.

He stood there a long time, waiting, but for what he was unsure. When finally the sound of the first birds returning woke him from his trance, Ethan turned away from the clearing and headed down the hill.

What Margaret Would Have Wanted

The first time I saw Earl, I reacted as you might expect of someone who'd come home to find a strange old man sitting in his back yard. I was getting out of my car when I noticed him sitting with his back against the cottage and he kind of spooked me. I had the impulse to chase him off.

So I did. Or at least I tried.

"Hey, get out of my back yard," I said.

"Who the hell are you?" he asked in a growl, his deeply lined face grimmacing in the sun. "And where's Margaret?"

* * *

Let me back up a bit because this story is about a house, or at least I think it is. A house with a cottage behind it. It's what the real estate man called a "mother-in-law-cottage," which I guess implies its purpose. The cottage sits along an alley that separates my property from the back of a row of stores whose fronts serve a busy street. I bought the place for the house, and the cottage came with the deal.

I'm single, and I'd been living in apartments throughout the decade since graduating from college. Apartment living had grown tiresome. I would move in somewhere and for a while it would be fine, but then for one reason or another I'd find myself moving again, maybe after a year, or even within a few months. There was the time I moved into a beautiful little place with a sliding door that opened out onto a lovely little park—my own private access—but it turned out the woman living above me was practicing for a black belt in judo and the incessant thudding of bodies on my ceiling unnerved me. I could hardly ask her to stop—after all, she'd been there first—but I couldn't stay.

I had frequently thought about buying a house of my own. I had enough money for a down payment since my father died and left me a small sum. My mother said on numerous occasions that investing it in property would be wise, and I got the feeling Dad had suggested this to her before he died. That was his way, to speak indirectly to me through her. Still, I found it difficult to commit to a venture as big as home ownership.

"It would be perfect for a family," she said to me one Saturday as we spoke on the phone. She'd called while I was eating breakfast. "A house is what a family needs."

"I don't have a family," I answered.

"I know," she said, "but maybe if you get a house . . ."

"It doesn't work that way, Mom. Women don't just go driving around on Friday nights searching out single men in appropriate family-sized houses. And anyway, I'd really have to meet the right woman if I was going to have a family." This was a conversation we'd had before and we simply repeated it every so often, as if by agreement. But this time my mother said something that caught me off guard, though it was a long time before I understood why she said it.

"Time can run out on you, Keith," she said. "You can have certain plans, something you figure you're going to do some day but you're . . . waiting for one reason or another. It can happen to any one of us, just anticipating that the perfect time will come. Then one day you look up and there isn't any more time."

* * *

Her comment didn't really hit me at first. It wasn't like I had the urge to go out and start a family that afternoon. But her words kept coming back to me. It took another year and two more apartments, but I finally decided to start looking at houses.

I remember in particular a string of nights when I lay awake in bed as the sounds of my neighbors' sad, clumsy lovemaking drifted through the walls. I realized the time had come. Besides, for no reason I could explain, I suddenly wanted to plant a garden.

* * *

I called Dan Rullison, a friend of the family, who had sold my parents their first house thirty-five years ago. I only meant to get information, but like a bird being sucked into a jet turbine engine, I was out riding the next day in his old beige Mercedes, cruising neighborhoods and looking at houses within my modest means.

"Now don't think you have to jump at the first thing," Dan reassured me as we drove along. I looked at him as he crouched over the wheel, his wiry hair and bushy eyebrows silvered like my father's had been. "No sir, there are plenty of houses for sale out there and you'll need to be patient to find just the right one, the one that speaks to you."

"How many are we going to look at this afternoon?" I asked.

"Well, I've got about five or six lined up, but we don't have to see them all today." He changed lanes and slowed to turn

right. "I want you to take your time, give things a good looking over, and let me answer any questions for you that I can. I
want you to know that I am personally interested in seeing you
get set up in something that's just right." He paused a moment
before adding, "I hope you don't mind but I gave your mother
a call after we spoke, and she asked me to do my best for you."

"I don't mind," I said. I could see my mother dancing a jig
around the kitchen in her floral print muumuu.

"Well, good. You know, I sold your folks their first house—
the very house you lived in, Keith."

We looked at six houses that day, and another six the day
after that. After two days of touring the marginal neighborhoods that contained the only houses for which I would quali-
fy, I began to rethink the whole idea. Some of the houses were
better than others, but most had one or another glaring flaw
that I couldn't get past. For starters, the house on Acorn Drive
was next to an apartment complex—not much different from
what I was leaving behind. The house on Burlington Avenue
had a front porch that leaned heavily to one side and the concrete steps were badly eroded. The Curtis Street house was
quaint, as if a squad of grannies had worked it over, but I didn't
want quaint. The house on Tindale Street, near the grade
school, looked fine from the outside, but one step inside and
I knew it had been home to generations of cranky male cats.
I almost got excited by the house on Garnet Street, with its
tasteful white paint job and beautiful blue spruce on the north
side, but all the rooms were small and cramped so that a feeling of claustrophobia overtook me after a few moments inside.

Dan was discouraged. I wasn't making it easy on him. But
then he showed me the house on Lincoln Street.

We had retired from searching for a couple of days, during
which time Dan called me and said he'd found several places

he thought were more along the lines of what I might want, and suggested we start out bright and early Friday morning. I agreed, deciding I owed myself another go. It didn't hurt that my neighbors, whose kitchen wall was also my kitchen wall, had gotten into a shouting match just before Dan called. I could hear the wife clear the dishes—not in the usual manner.

Dan showed up Friday wearing a bright yellow sweater and an attitude to match. Clearly, he thought I needed a different kind of handling.

"Hope you're ready, Keith," he said loudly as he escorted me back to the car. "I've got something really special to show you today. There's a little place over on Mayhew that has a hot tub on the back deck—just what every bachelor needs, right?"

"You've been talking to my mother again," I said.

"Well, Keith, I can't tell a lie. She did call to see how things were going. I told here we were making progress."

"So was the hot tub her idea?"

Dan smiled. "Not in so many words," he said, "but just between us guys, you know the ladies love a little romance. A nice dinner, a bottle of wine, and a hot tub under stars." He nudged me in the ribs with his elbow. I forced a laugh. He laughed, too, and we got in the car.

Dan tuned the radio to a station I'd never heard before—playing a vaguely familiar pop song from the early sixties. It was clearly meant to be cheerful, but something about the beige Mercedes, the yellow sweater, and nameless song bleating through the tinny speakers seemed terribly depressing at that moment.

"But before we go to this place I'm thinking of, there's one other property on the way I thought we'd just drive past—nothing fancy, we can just drive on past and if you think you want a quick look, we can stop, go in, look around. It's on the way."

He steered his Mercedes into the flow of traffic and turned
south on the busy boulevard that swept past my apartment
building. We hadn't gone far when he turned again, this time
onto Lincoln Street, just one block off the thoroughfare. We
pulled up at the curb in front of a white house with beaten
wood siding. It was in need of a paint job and the overgrown
junipers out front were monstrous. The house had a peaked
roof and around the side yard there were orange poppies nodding in the breeze. I could make out what looked like a large
garage in the back, at the end of a driveway that consisted of
two narrow strips of concrete with a weedy patch of grass between. A huge silver maple shaded the front yard.

"Well, this is it. I just thought we'd take a look." Dan paused,
waiting for my reaction. He didn't cut the engine. I was checking out the house. After a moment he said, "Okay, listen, let's
move on because I think you're going to really like this other
place . . ."

"Wait a minute," I said. There was something appealing
about the house, despite the shabbiness. "Can we take a look
inside?"

"Sure," Dan said, raising his eyebrows. "We can do that." He
cut the engine and we got out and walked up the front steps.
Dan fiddled with the combination lock that hung from the
door handle, finally managing to remove the key from the attached box. He inserted it in the lock, opened the door, and
then stepped back.

"Be my guest," he said.

The house was different than the others I'd seen. As soon
as I stepped in it felt welcoming, comfortable. I made my way
around the living room, noticing the small fireplace. I explored
the kitchen—small but inviting, with a row of glass-fronted
cabinets. Along the north side of the house there were a se-

ries of bedrooms, one larger than the others and featuring its own bathroom with a claw-foot tub and antique fixtures. The window opened onto the back yard and I went to the sill and looked out. What I'd taken for a garage was really a cottage, separate from the house itself but clearly part of the property.

"Dan," I called out, and then again, louder.

"Yeah, Keith, right here." He came into the bathroom. "What's up?" And then before I could answer him, he said, "Oh, I see you've found it. The cottage."

"Is it part of this property?"

"It sure is. Built by the same person who built the house. These are pretty typical, you know, called a mother-in-law cottage. Kind of makes sense, don't you think?"

"Can I take a look?"

"Let's go," he said, and stepped briskly toward the kitchen where he searched through a drawer until he'd found a ring with more keys on it.

We went out the back door, down the steps, and across the weedy lawn, past a small, derelict garden plot, and up to the door of the cottage. I peered in the window while he worked at the lock, trying a series of keys until one clicked and the door opened.

Inside was a modest but self-contained living space. It had a gas stove, a bathtub (out in the open), and some simple furniture including a table, two chairs, a bed, and a desk by the window. A hot water heater stood in the far corner. I also noticed an old record player next to the desk and a crate of LPs of some ancient vintage. A layer of dust covered everything.

"This is very interesting," I said. "I like this very much." Something about the cottage captured my imagination, though I couldn't put my finger on it.

"Well, you'll have to buy the house to get it," Dan said jokingly. "They're a package."

"I like the house, too," I said. "But I'm thinking I could put up friends and family in this little place when they come to visit. It's kind of funky—my mother would be very comfortable staying here."

"That's right," Dan chimed in. "Or a mother-in-law, maybe."

I let that slide and said, "Heck, I could even rent it out, if necessary."

"I suppose you could," he said.

"Maybe I ought to buy it," I said.

So I did.

* * *

Later, when I looked back on it, I think the cottage was what really sold me, and that's ironic considering what happened shortly thereafter. I had long feared that by settling into a house I'd be initiating a chain reaction that would turn me inside out. It wasn't the house that did it; I realize that now. Changes were coming anyway. Change is always coming. Earl, the old man, taught me that. He taught me you can't just huddle inside your life and hope the wind will forget you're there and just blow past you. He also taught me it's best to face changes head-on because there's dignity in that, and it can be enough to get you through.

* * *

Here are the things I did to fix up the house.

I scraped off all the old paint, borrowed a friend's spray gun, and laid on a layer of the best primer and couple of layers of paint in the shades I'd liked so much: a muted grey-green, with the trim in a tasteful deep green and white.

I dug up the hideous juniper bushes out front and carted

them to the dump.

I pulled up the carpets and resurfaced the wood floors.

I put in a dishwasher.

I put in a gas stove.

I cleaned out the fireplace—a brutal chore.

I painted the interior, stem to stern, in understated colors like bone white and tan, taking care to strip and re-finish the woodwork around the doorways. The effect was handsome.

I bought some furniture that seemed to fit—an oak dining table with matching chairs and a large, L-shaped sofa for the living room.

I did all these things, and through the summer quite a few more, until my house truly became my home. Still, every time I went out back to the cottage to contemplate repairs and changes, I came away feeling I should do nothing at all to it. One morning I took a cup of coffee out back and sat inside at the small table, looking out at my house, freshly painted and catching the rays of early sun on the gables. The air in the cottage was cool and dry, the quiet remarkable. It felt good to be there and my coffee tasted richer as I sipped it and gazed through the open door.

The truth was obvious: the little hut didn't really need anything. It was complete, and I was content to leave it just as it was.

* * *

I had been in the house just over six months when I came home that day and found the old man sitting with his back against the locked door of the cottage, a greasy bundle of clothes tied loosely and resting beside him. He had his shoes off and he was paring his fingernails with a pocket knife. For a minute, I thought I'd made a mistake and pulled into the wrong driveway. But there was no mistaking it. That was my house, and my cottage, and there was a grubby old street person sitting there as if he were waiting for me to return.

"Who the hell are you?" he said, "And where's Margaret?"

"Who?" I asked.

"Margaret, Margaret, Margaret. Are you deaf? Margaret."

I told him I didn't know who Margaret was. He got stiffly to his feet and glowered at me. I worried for a moment that he was a nut case and the little penknife in his hand might actually be dangerous.

"I'm talking about Margaret. Don't give me some story about 'don't know this or that.' She's the woman that lives here, in this here house. And who the hell are you, anyway? I know you ain't one of her grandkids." He squinted at me and took a step closer.

I couldn't help myself. I let go a nervous laugh. Having gotten over my initial shock, I could see the old man was an odd bird, quite possibly deranged, but despite his rough manner, he posed no real threat. I came around from the side of my car and approached him.

"Pardon me," I said. "My name's Keith, and I bought this house last spring."

The old man stopped what he was doing and looked at me, hard. His lips tightened up and he squinted. "Where's Margaret?" he repeated one last time, his voice stripped of its edges now and coming out in a wheeze. It was then I remembered what Dan had told me at the closing. The house had belonged to a woman, the wife of the man who had built it many years ago. She'd lived there alone for over thirty years after her husband died, and some time in March she'd passed away, having lived to the age of ninety.

"Margaret's dead," I said to the old man. "I'm afraid she died last spring."

I should have realized the effect it might have before I said it. The old man shook his head, his shoulders slumped, and his eyes brimmed suddenly. "No," he said. "No, that can't be. She looked fine when I left. She gave me this . . . here . . . she gave me this." He began rummaging in his coat pocket until he came up with a book, which he handed to me. It was a thin volume of poems by Percy Bysshe Shelley. I absentmindedly opened to the first poem, "Ode to the West Wind."

"She gave that to me," the old man repeated, his voice going weaker with each syllable. "I told her I'd return it. How am I going to do that?"

I didn't know what to say. I looked at him again, saw his filthy garments, the sparse white hair that stood out from his head in all directions, the grizzled beard sprouting along his jaw. I saw his lips trembling. It dawned on me what must be going on.

"You wait right here," I said, and turned to the house. Inside, I found the key to the cottage and came back out. The old man was slumped against the wall when I got back, his face a mask of pain and confusion. I opened the door and helped him inside. He moved toward the bed, where he sat down and began removing his boots. Then, ever so slowly, he opened up the drawer of the desk and without looking he took a weathered case from the drawer, removed his bent glasses, and stowed them inside.

I learned that Earl had lived in the cottage for a long time. Always for just half the year—the cold half—and that was why he showed up that September evening. He was returning home after wandering who knows where all summer long. He never said exactly how long he'd called the cottage home, but I got the idea it was decades ago when he had first arrived, which explained the stacks of old magazines that sat on the shelf by the bed, the colorful covers dulled with age and dust. I had gone to move them once, shortly after I'd first moved in, but for some reason I couldn't bring myself to disturb the pile. It seemed ancient, like an artifact in a museum display.

But I came to understand that these things belonged to Earl. This cottage was his home.

That first night I sat with Earl a little while, listened to him reminisce about Margaret and the kindness she had shown him over the years. By the time I left him to sleep in the cottage, I understood Earl would be staying for a while. I brought him a change of clothes the next morning, along with a bar of soap, a towel, and a razor from my cabinet. He didn't use the razor, preferring the dusting of white stubble that never seemed to grow longer. He was small and frail, and my shirt and pants hung loosely on his frame. But once he was cleaned up, Earl didn't look half bad—a little like my own grandpa, in fact, a man whose skin had taken on the same tough, brown hue from his years spent working on a ranch in New Mexico.

* * *

I never really thought about asking him to leave. I wasn't using the cottage, anyway. My offers to friends and family to come visit had not, apparently, been taken very seriously. I don't understand how it happened that I had become estranged from my family, but so it goes. My older brother Mark, who lives in Vancouver, hadn't been in touch in years, and all I knew of his recent life I'd gathered from my mother. My sister, Lisa, wrote back to say that she and her husband Greg and their three kids would love to come for a visit, and she'd keep it in mind, but that was a line I'd heard before, and even though I told her I had a house—and a guest house—I sensed her enthusiasm wasn't genuine.

My mother said she'd visit, of course, and I knew she would eventually, but I figured it would come as a huge surprise. That was the way she liked to do things, all of a sudden.

I called her one Sunday morning to update her about the work I'd done on the house. "I've really been fixing things up," I said. "It hardly looks like the same place."

"That's good, Keith," she said. "I knew you'd thrive in your own place. I can't wait to see it. All I have is the snapshot you sent me a while back. I bet it looks completely different now, with a new coat of paint and all that."

"Well, all except for the cottage," I said.

"You mean you didn't paint the cottage?"

"No."

"Why not?" she persisted.

"Well, it didn't seem to need it. I like it the way it is."

"Surely, now, it doesn't match the house," she said. "You want it to match the house, don't you?"

"It's okay, Mom. Really." I wanted her to understand it was my place, and this was a kind of statement. "Besides," I said, "there's more to it than that."

There was a pause. She was waiting for me to finish the thought. I couldn't think of any way to explain the presence of Earl that wouldn't make her think I'd really gone over the edge. A homeless man living in my cottage. She would never understand.

"What exactly do you mean?" she asked, more curious than accusatory. So I told her. I just came out and explained the whole circumstance—how I'd found Earl that night, how he seemed so lost when I told him about Margaret, maybe the only friend he had, whose death had occasioned the opportunity for me to buy the place. I told her about how he was no trouble, really, and he didn't ask for anything except to have a warm place to stay.

"And I don't have any use for the cottage anyway, at least not now," I said. "I've got plenty of room in the house, and nobody has come to visit yet. I don't expect anybody in winter."

"You're upset about your sister, aren't you?"

"No," I said. "She and Stuart have plenty else going on. I'm sure they'll make it eventually."

"I'll make it, too," she said. "I want to visit and see your new place. And I look forward to meeting Mr. . . . what did you say his name was?"

"Earl," I said.

"I look forward to meeting Earl."

It wasn't the main reason she came to visit, of course, but I didn't know at the time.

* * *

I got used to the idea of Earl living in the cottage; it seemed natural. It was, after all, his home. In a sense, his claim was more valid than any I could make. We began talking occasionally, and the tales he told me were laced with references to this neighborhood, to times before I was even born. He knew many of the neighbors by name. I even saw Mrs. Gresham from across the street wave hello to him one morning, which was more than she did for me. I got used to the idea that Earl was meant to be a tenant, and found it comforting, in an odd way, to pull in at night and see a light in the window of the cottage.

He didn't ask for much. I let him keep the clothes I'd given him and I tossed in a couple other pairs of pants, a shirt that had always fit me too snugly, and even a pair of boots I didn't use. He always accepted these things in his gruff but gracious manner. I noticed that he kept the cottage clean inside, sweep-

ing and mopping the floor every Sunday and cleaning out the
tub, the kitchen sink, and the toilet.

"Can I borrow your bucket," he'd say, standing at the back
porch steps. "I've got some cleaning up to do."

I would go and get the bucket and cleaning supplies and
give them to him.

"I'll return them when I'm through," he'd say, always the
same way. "Thank you kindly." And then he'd shuffle off, cart-
ing the materials back to the cottage.

If I invited him to share a meal with me, which I did more
often as time went by, he would always accept. He would always bow his head and say grace, mumbling quietly. The first
time, when I didn't follow his lead, he stopped and glared at
me. It registered soon enough, and I clasped my hands and
bowed my head. After a second he continued.

As a way of being gracious he would usually invite me
back to the cottage after a meal, where we would sit and talk
late into the night. I learned quite a bit about him and I also
learned who Margaret had been. She and Earl had a long history together. I often wondered whether they had been closer
than he let on, but finally I realized that had never been the
case. Earl provided her the services of gardener and handyman
that she so desperately needed after the death of her husband,
and she, in return, gave him a place to stay and food to eat
when the weather turned cold and put an end to his summer
rambles.

"At one time," Earl told me, "I used to go out and find work
in the summers. It wasn't just wandering. I'd go up to Idaho,
pick potatoes, or east to Nebraska and work harvesting corn.
I wasn't always just wandering. But then I got old, too old for
work, and besides, they took to hiring immigrant field workers
and I couldn't find any place that would have me."

"So what did you do?" I asked.

"I just wandered," he said, and that was all he said.

* * *

Earl had some strange habits. I found this out because sometimes, even though I knew I shouldn't, I would sit at my kitchen table and watch him. One of his rituals was what I call The Dizzy Astronomer. On new moon nights, when the sky was clear and black, Earl could sometimes be found standing out in the cold night air, turning slow circles in the back yard, his neck craned and his eyes fixed on the stars.

I never knew what it was about. Maybe he just liked constellations.

Another time I saw him standing on the porch of the cottage, as still as a statue, his face pressed against the wall. It seemed a strange and unnatural posture to me, especially considering that he held that way, absolutely still, for sometimes fifteen or twenty minutes—and then I saw it. A hummingbird flitting about the branches of a nearby tree until it worked up the courage and came to sip sugar water from the feeder he'd affixed to a spot just inches from where he'd rested his head.

* * *

My mother finally came to visit in mid-January. She said she couldn't stand traveling during the holiday season, and anyway, she'd spent the holidays with Lisa and her family.

I met her at the airport. When she first came up the ramp from the plane, I barely recognized her. At first, it was the difference in her hair; she'd always worn it long but now it was cut short, and any trace of the rich brown color it once had was gone. It caught me off guard. I stepped forward and put my arms around her; she seemed so small.

"It's so good to see you, Keith," she said, and embraced me again. "You look so good, honey."

"Thanks, Mom. You look good, too," I said, hoping my voice didn't betray me.

"Well, you better say that," she said, holding me at arm's length.

"Your hair," I said.

A look of consternation came over her face. I remembered being a kid, and when that look came over her face I knew she was disappointed in me for something. "Go ahead," she said. "You can say so if you don't like it."

"It's not that," I said, stalling. "It's just so different. You've got to give me a moment to get used to it." But what I was really thinking was that she'd lost weight, and how frail her shoulders felt when I put my arms around her.

We went right from the airport to a little café downtown, where I often had lunch with friends from work, and we talked of many things: Lisa's youngest daughter, now taking piano lessons at five years old. My brother Mark's pending transfer from Vancouver to St. Louis—a bad move, I opined, to which my mother nodded. My mother seemed in especially good spirits, and by the time the meal was over I began to realize how excited I was for the main event: showing off my house.

It wasn't until we were almost there that Earl crossed my mind. I pictured Earl turning circles in the back yard under the cover of stars and I only hoped my mother would understand I'd come to feel responsible for the old guy.

* * *

"Oh Keith," she said, as we pulled up in front of the house. "This is so nice. I can hardly believe it." She looked over at me, beaming, and then she patted my leg lovingly, like mothers will do. "You've settled down."

"Well, I'm part of the way there," I said. "So far, it's just me in the house."

"You and Earl," she said, mischievously.

"Okay," I said. "Me and Earl."

I gave her the grand tour. I showed her the upstairs, the redecorated kitchen and bath, the spare but fashionable furniture I'd put in the living room. I even lit a fire in the fireplace to show her how it worked. I carried her bag to the guest bedroom and put it on the bed next to the set of towels I'd placed there earlier that day. When I turned around I noticed she'd found her way down to the basement, so I followed, pointing out the finished portion (a rumpus room, she called it), and the unfinished portion that I hoped some day to turn into an additional bedroom, assuming the need might arise.

"This is all very nice, Keith," she said. "And what about the cottage? Do I get to see that?"

"Uh, not right now." For some reason, I'd become increasingly apprehensive since I realized she was coming and I wanted to hold off on the whole Earl thing until the right moment.

"As you wish," she said. "Let's go up and have a cup of tea, shall we?"

* * *

I had just finished cooking dinner—I'd had to practically fight my mother away from the skillet and cupboard, insisting I could do it—when there was a knock at the back door.

Earl.

I was hurrying to put the salmon fillet on the table before the side dishes cooled, and my hands were covered with butter. I quickly grabbed a towel to wipe them off but before I could manage it my mother jumped to her feet and hurried over to the door.

"Mom . . ." I said, but I was too late. She turned the knob and pulled the door open to reveal Earl, standing with his hat in his hand like some Depression-era unfortunate finally having made it to the front of the soup line.

"'Scuse me ma'am," he said in his most polite, scratchy voice, "I'm awful sorry to interrupt, I was just hoping to have a word with Keith if I might."

"Well you must be Earl," my mother said, and she took him by the arm and led him inside. "I'm Angela, Keith's mother."

"I'm pleased to meet you, ma'am," Earl said, bowing his head slightly and shuffling his feet.

"Why you're just in time for dinner, Earl," she said. "Would you care to join us?"

"Oh, I couldn't do that ma'am," Earl said, and he shot a quick look over her shoulder at me. I was no more in control of the situation than he was, though, so I merely shrugged and nodded to the table.

"Oh, but I insist," my mother said. "Keith, you set another place for this gentleman." She led him to the table and took her seat next to him. His eyes grew big as silver dollars when I put out the salmon and uncovered the steaming pot of rice.

And so it went, my mother serving as master of ceremonies, Earl playing the gracious but rough-around-the-edges bumpkin, and me content to keep the food and wine flowing and listen to the conversation unwind. At first Earl was reluctant to say much, but his resolve gave way under the relentless flow of my mother's questions until I began to learn things about the man, and about Margaret, the old woman of the house, that I had never guessed.

It turned out Margaret had come from a family of Wobblies—that is, her parents were labor organizers for the Industrial Workers of the World in its heyday just before World War

I. Her father, a lumberman, favored the socialist side of the or-
ganization when it split in the 1920s, and though he was later in-
dicted for fraud he was acquitted of the charges and withdrew
from the leadership. Still, Margaret's husband was a young lumberman himself, and after they married and built the house,
Earl said, they continued to use it as a gathering place through
the thirties and forties for workers with socialist leanings who
met there to debate the coming of the workers' paradise.

"I wasn't around then, you see," Earl said. "I didn't show up
around here until '59, and by then her husband Ned was gone
and Margaret was all alone."

"So was it through this connection with the IWW that you came
to know her?" my mother asked, continuing to ply Earl for answers.

"No, ma'am," Earl said, shaking his head and looking down
at his plate. "I was looking for work, you know, any kind of
odd job I could find, and not having much luck at it, I don't
mind saying. I was walking down this here street one spring
morning, my belly empty as it could be, when I saw this woman leaning heavily on a spade in her back yard. She'd been dig-
ging, and was resting, so I thought, but then she kind of fell
to the ground, not fainting, but just kind of exhausted. Well,
I rushed over to help her, and when I'd gotten her inside and
fetched a cool drink, I went back out and set to work spading
that little plot she'd set out. Now I didn't expect nothing from
her, I just did it. It seemed the right thing to do."

My mother nodded her assent, and I offered Earl some
more vegetables and little more wine, which he accepted.

"So what happened then?" my mother asked.

"Well, like I say, I set to that job and finished just about the
time daylight was fading. I was knocking off my boots and I
thought to ask the woman where she wanted me to put the
spade and the wheelbarrow, when she came out on the back

porch," and at this Earl wheeled slowly and looked out the back door. He stopped talking, and it seemed for a moment he might be seeing Margaret again, standing in a blue apron on the back steps, her hair pulled up in a bun and the setting sun reflecting off the white house around her.

"She had a plate of biscuits," Earl said, his voice suddenly smoother than I'd ever heard it, "hot from the oven, with a little crock of butter and another crock of honey. I was so hungry, I felt weak in the knees, you know. But she brought that food out and we sat on the back porch and ate together. It was the best meal I ever had—'cept of course for your cooking tonight, ma'am," he said.

"Oh, well thank you Earl, but I can't take credit for something I haven't done," she said, and grinned at me. "This fine feast was made by my son."

Earl glanced up at me, and I returned his smile of gratitude. "Did you get enough to eat?" I asked him.

"I certainly did," he said. "Thank you."

The conversation went on a long time. We moved to the living room, and at first Earl was uncomfortable, unsure of where to sit. The furniture wasn't what he was used to. Eventually he took a seat on the couch and after a few more glasses of wine—I'd opened a third bottle—he began to settle his bony frame back into it until he looked like a little boy in his father's chair. My mother seemed extraordinarily interested in Earl, in his story, and she kept on with her questions about Margaret, the house, and the history of the neighborhood. I was content to listen and pour the wine. We found out about the fire that had burned down the string of stores behind the house in 1961, and about the time Earl found a little baby, abandoned in a cardboard box at the edge of the alley. Margaret had taken in the child until a home was found across town, and the little girl grew up and sometimes came by to visit and help Margaret with shopping and cooking, until she met a man and moved away to Montana.

Somewhere along in the evening, with the sound of Earl's scruffy voice in my ears, I fell off to sleep, and awakened in the dark to my mother stroking my arm and softly repeating my name. "Keith, come on now, it's time for bed." I shook the sleep from my head and slowly stood up.

"What time is it?" I asked.

"Well, it would be about three a.m.," she replied. "Earl and I have had a fine conversation. He's a nice old gentleman." After a pause, she looked me in the eye and said, "It's kind of you to let him stay here, Keith."

"It seemed the only thing to do, " I said. "He's no trouble, really." My mother nodded her agreement. "Do you need anything else?" I asked groggily.

She shook her head, kissed me lightly on the cheek, and padded off to her bedroom.

* * *

That was how it went during her visit. I had the first few days off from work, and we spent the evenings talking with Earl, who always seemed to show up about the time the last serving dish hit the table at dinner time. The one night he didn't come knocking at the door, my mother went out back to the cottage and retrieved him. She did the cooking after I went back to work, and it only took a few days for me to notice that I was putting on pounds. And more than that, I was getting used to having her around. She seemed somehow to have shed some years since I'd seen her last—it wasn't just the new hairdo, or the fact that she seemed slimmer and lighter on her feet. There was a new energy about her that I couldn't quite place, energy to stay up late at night talking with Earl long after I'd gone to bed. She slept in the afternoons while I was at work, and in the evenings after dinner we'd repeat the ritual: wine and conversation around the fireplace.

Several times I woke to find the living room deserted. The first couple of times I just dragged myself off to bed, assuming they had done likewise and decided to let me lie where I was, "sleeping like a baby," as my mother would put it the next morning. But the last time it had happened, I was clearing my wine glass to the kitchen when I looked out the back window and saw the light on in the cottage. Against my better judgment—for I had no right to do it—I sneaked out the front door and around the back of the house, approaching the cottage from an angle. I peered through a gap in the drapes, careful to keep myself concealed.

There they were, sitting at the tiny table in Earl's cottage, laughing and drinking wine. I hurried away, ashamed of myself for spying on them, but deeply pleased to see my mother and Earl enjoying the moment. It made me aware, in a way I had never been, that I myself had no one with whom I shared that kind of time.

* * *

My mother stayed more than a month, and near the end of her time with me she began, finally, to show signs of weariness. "Those late nights will kill you," I said jokingly one morning over breakfast, as we were talking about her pending departure.

She flinched a little at my words, and I immediately regretted saying it.

"I'm sorry, mom. It's none of my business," I said.

She reached across the table and took my hand. "No, Keith,

it's not that. You know at my age there's nobody I have to an-swer to. Earl and I are just, well, kind of contemporaries, you might say. He reminds me an awful lot of your father in some ways, and I miss your father still."

"I can understand that," I said. "But I never thought of Earl as anything like Dad at all."

"Well, not on the surface," she said. "But underneath that grizzled exterior, he's a kind and gentle old man. I think more than anything, I love his stories. They're fascinating, and they take me back to a time I thought I'd forgotten forever." She paused here, and I felt her hand tighten on mine. When she looked up, I saw her eyes moistening.

"Keith, there's something I've got to tell you. I've been keep-ing it from you all this time, and after all, it's part of the reason I came out to see you because I wanted to talk to you in person, not over the phone."

"What is it, Mom?" I could hear in the change of tone that something was wrong, very wrong.

"Keith, last spring I noticed I'd been feeling a little under the weather, so I went to see the doctor. You know, it didn't seem anything serious, it was just that I felt run-down, like I couldn't keep my energy level up. I also was having some pains in my abdomen, and I found I was getting a little light-headed at times. So I went to see the doctor."

"What did he say?"

"Not much, at first. They ran some tests, you know, the usu-al thing, and for a while there was no sign of anything wrong. But I wasn't getting better, so they tested me for a few other problems. And they found one." A chill passed over me when she said this, and I looked up at her face, now drawn and tight. She looked more frail than ever, and it dawned on me that I'd been right to think there might be something wrong.

"I'm afraid I've got cancer, Keith." She said this with courage, and I felt something give way inside me. "It's in my liver. You understand, this isn't something that gets better," she said. "There are treatments, but you understand, my time is limited."

There is no adequate reply when your mother tells you she's dying, so I said nothing at that moment. I got up, went to the sink, and refilled the already full kettle with water. When I turned around, I saw her, again transformed, smiling brightly and looking past me to the back door, where Earl stood shuffling his feet. In his hand was a wooden box.

* * *

Earl gave my mother a small but beautiful collection of pins, amulets, and bracelets that had once belonged to Margaret. She had put them in the cottage for safekeeping, he said, and since he'd found out she was gone, he'd wondered what to do with them. "I don't know as she has any family in the area," Earl said, "or else I'd try to get these to them. But I don't think so. I've been keeping them under the floorboards in the cottage, and now I think you ought to have them."

"Thank you, Earl," she said. "It's very kind of you to think of me this way."

"It's what Margaret would have wanted," Earl said.

My mother and Earl sat together at the table looking at each piece, with Earl filling in any detail he could about them. All trace of my mother's weariness was gone from her face, and as she pieced over the jewelry and trinkets, she looked like a young girl again, her eyes bright and the yellowish cast of her skin, which I had noticed in days before but chose to ignore, now somehow gone. Or at least I chose to see it that way.

* * *

She left the next day. I took her to the airport. I asked Earl if
he wanted to go, but he just shook his head, said he'd say a
proper good-bye to my mother before she left. They embraced
awkwardly, on the top step of the back porch, and Earl retired
quickly to his cottage and shut the door.

As we drove to the airport, I struggled to find a way to
ask my mother when I would see her again. How long did
she have? Could I even ask such a thing, and would she even
know? Finally, as we sat at the gate waiting for her flight to
board, I could see no other way, so I put the question directly.

With great poise, she told me that her time was short, but
she didn't know exactly how short. "I may have six months,
son," she said. "Maybe a little more. I'm not going to take the
treatments my doctor has offered, as they will do little to extend my time and the side effects are . . . well, I have no desire
to drag this out, you understand. I'm ready."

"But mom," I protested, "you can't just give up."

She reached out and touched my cheek gently. "Keith, I'm
not giving up. I just want to go on my own terms. My plan is
to visit my children and spend as much time with them as I
can. I'm sorry I didn't tell you as soon as I arrived, so that we
could talk more. I know this is hard on you."

I felt myself going hollow inside. For the second time in as
many days, I couldn't think of what to say.

"I'm going on a short cruise," she said, "leaving as soon as I
get back. Marie and I—you remember Marie, right? She's the
little Italian woman down the street—we're going to the Ca-
ribbean. We're going to live it up. I'll be gone until late March,
but as soon as I get back, I'll call you. Lisa is thinking about
getting the whole family together at her place. Will you come?"

I nodded.

"Keith, don't be sad," she said. "You have so much going for you now. That house, it's a beautiful house, honey. It really is. I like what you've done with it. And it's so kind, you taking care of Earl like that. A lesser man might have tossed him out when he found him at the cottage. You're very kind, and he might not say it, but he appreciates what you're doing."

I could still find no words, so I hugged her and held on for a few moments. The attendant at the gate announced final boarding, and I moved to get her carry-on bag.

"There's just one more thing," my mother said. "Now that you've got that fine house, Keith, get yourself a nice girl. Life's a whole lot sweeter when you've got someone to share it with."

* * *

And I did just that. It wasn't like I deliberately went out on a mission, but it so happened that a woman I once knew came back into my life. I had dated Kim for several months, but as things were getting serious she took a transfer to Los Angeles and I had assumed it was a sign. But that is another story, for another time. What happened with Earl is more interesting by far.

After my mother's visit, Earl was different. The winter was gradually turning over, the days growing longer and warmer. I saw less of Earl, and he was gone most days, coming home late, even after I'd gone to bed. One evening, I was walking with Kim and we saw Earl in City Park, spinning as he often did in my back yard, his eyes fixed on some celestial point, his arms flared ever so slightly as if he might ascend somehow.

"Isn't that Earl?" Kim asked.

"How many other spinning men do we know?"

"Not a one," she said. She took my hand and we both slowed down to watch him for a moment. "He's a strange old man, but I kind of like him."

"My mother did, too," I said. "Must be something in the old goat's blood that drives women crazy."

"I don't know about that," she said. "It's just . . . he's interesting."

* * *

One evening, in late March, when the last wet snows were falling and melting, falling and melting, I saw Earl gathering his things inside the cottage. I'd gone back to check on him because I'd heard some banging coming from inside his place, and when I stepped through the open door, there was Earl, peeling back one of the floorboards. He looked up sheepishly at me and began to apologize.

"Now I'm sorry to be doing this," Earl said. "I promise, I'll put it back in place so as no one would know it was ever pulled up."

"That's okay, Earl," I assured him. There isn't anybody going to be back in here anyway but me."

"Well, aren't you going to have your family visit some time?" he asked.

I shrugged and told him the offer was still standing, but the only person I could see making the trip again would be my mother. I told him my whole family was planning to gather in St. Louis later in the spring.

"How is your mother," Earl asked.

"She's well," I told him. "As well as can be expected."

Earl got up from what he was doing and took a seat at his small table. He pulled out a drawer, removed rolling papers and tobacco, and commenced to roll himself a cigarette. I joined him at the table but declined his offer of a smoke. I watched as his wizened fingers moved deftly with the paper and leaves, rolling the cigarette up neatly with only one hand, raising it and lighting it quickly.

"I'm awful sorry about your mother," Earl finally said to me. "I have been meaning to say that to you, but I couldn't find the right time, so I guess this is it."

"I appreciate that, Earl," I said.

"She's a fine woman, your mother," he said. "If I were a few years younger, or maybe if I were a real gentleman who wouldn't embarrass her with the question, I'd think to ask her to marry me."

I admit, I was surprised to hear the old man say it, but I tried not to show my surprise.

"I really am sorry that she's sick," Earl said. "It ain't right. First Margaret, and now your mother going. There ain't enough good women out there as it is."

"She is a fine woman," I said.

"And there's another one I forgot to mention," Earl said, a little sparkle in his eye. He got up from his seat and went back to the board he'd been working on. "That young lady you've taken up with is awful pretty," he said, grinning over his shoulder at me.

I laughed at his remark and he went back to working on the board a little more, finally getting it completely up from the floor. Then he laid himself flat on the floor, with his left arm completely extended under the boards, and groped about for a few moments. I watched, wondering just what he was trying to retrieve. Finally, he withdrew and I saw he had another box, much like the one he'd given to my mother. Earl got to his feet slowly and made his way back to the table, brushing off dust and dirt from box's lid before putting it down in front of me.

I looked up at him and he thrust out his grizzled chin at me, indicating I was to open the box up. I fumbled with the old latch for a moment before managing to draw it up and open the lid. In contrast to the dusty exterior, the interior was lined with plush red velvet, and lying inside was a beautiful necklace, a silver chain with a teardrop-shaped piece of onyx the size of my thumb hanging low.

"What's this?" I asked.

"It's Margaret's," Earl said.

"Would you like me to send it to my mother?" I asked.

"Not exactly," Earl said.

*　*　*

The next morning, Earl was gone. I'd gotten up early, fixed a good breakfast of pancakes, bacon, coffee, and toast, which was usually enough to bring Earl out from his lodging. When he didn't come up the back steps, I went out to get him. I found the cabin door locked and there was no answer when I knocked. I went in and got the key from the drawer inside, went out back again, and slowly opened the cottage up.

"Earl, " I called. "Earl, you sleeping?" There was no reply. I pulled back the drape to let the morning sun in and found the place immaculately cleaned. There was no sign of the old man.

I suppose I knew he would be going, the same way I sensed he'd be back again when fall brought a nip to the night air and an old man on the road needed a place to stay.

"So, the old bird has flown the nest."

I turned and saw Kim standing in the sun-framed door of the cottage. She's a small woman, with long black hair and hands so delicate they might belong to a child. "I was just passing by," she said, "and I smelled something good. You wouldn't happen to have enough breakfast for two, would you?"

I walked over, kissed her, and nodded. "Plenty of it," I said, and picking up from the table the little box Earl had given me the night before, I closed the cottage door behind us.

The Lake

I've always known the lake as a dangerous place. When I was a boy, my mother used to say the same thing. "Don't play around there," she used to tell me, "It'll swallow you up some day." I didn't listen—I was always down to the shore skipping stones, skirting around the willows along the east side outlet that sticks like a tongue into the woods. A few times my friend Hal and I even took out the old canoe we found by what was left of Stoddard's cabin. One of us would paddle, the other one would bail with a rusty tin can, and we'd stay close to shore because we were scared stiff something bad would happen if we didn't. We were probably right.

I don't know why but it always seems overcast down at the lake. Even on sunny summer days when you draw up close to the water, the air feels a good ten degrees cooler and the light dims as though a cloud has crossed between you and the sun. The water always changes its color, but most of the time it's a murky, green-gray color, and when you look down into it, you can't tell if the damn thing is bottomless or just some over-sized mud puddle. Some say it's because the lake is basically a wide spot in the river, so the natural current keeps stirring up silt from the bottom. Even in the shallows you can't see the rocks.

That's why this whole thing bothers me. Nobody knows whether the Riordan boy really drowned in the lake last month. We searched, and I mean searched—we walked every inch of the shore, walked downstream to the dam, but there was no sign of Jack's body. We even had a team from Clay County Sheriff's department come over with scuba gear and spend four days dragging the place. The body still hasn't turned up, and I've begun to wonder if it ever will.

Pete Riordon says he's not so sure his boy went down in the lake. He's always doubted it ever since the night he called us. It was Halloween and my wife and I were cleaning up the dinner dishes when the phone rang.

"Ed, I need your help," Pete said, and his voice was quivering something terrible. "We think Jack's drowned in the lake, over by the outlet side. The Sheriff's over there now with some men, but we need volunteers to help."

"What in God's name was he doing out on the lake," I asked, and I immediately regretted saying it. "Pete, this is awful. I'm sorry. What happened?"

There was a short silence, and when he spoke again, I heard that same something in his voice. It was panic. "I don't know, Ed, I don't know. I hope it's all a mistake, I hope he's just off somewhere. But I don't think so. Shiela Nelson was out by the dock and said she saw Jack take off in the outboard about dusk. We just found it, abandoned, bumping up against the spillway gate."

I didn't know what to say. I told him I'd be right down. "Oh, one more thing," Pete added. "Bring your hip waders along."

The drive out to the lake took longer than it ever had. I had to take it slow, with kids out everywhere. I'd come up on a group of them, scuttling along the sidewalk, all suited up like devils and witches and what have you—I don't mind saying it spooked me bad to see them, given the circumstances and all.

As I pulled over the rise and down the dirt road to the spillway gate, I could see a half-dozen patrol cars with their spotlight beams sweeping over the water by the shore. The boat had been secured to the gate and was bobbing a bit. Several men were already down in the shallows in their hip waders, and so was Jack's mother, Maura. She's not the type given to hysterics. Pete told me later she was the first person there, and when he arrived, she'd already put her boots on and had walked the narrow cement draw at the lip of the spillway to look for Jack.

We were there all night. We tried fanning out and walking the shore, and then the sheriff had us join hands and walk out from the shore as far as we could go. Moving in that fashion, we covered nearly a quarter mile on each side of the spillway by sunrise. I remember the tenseness as we walked through the dark, chilly water that pressed the rubber waders to my legs and finally spilled over and sloshed around my feet. It was no use to strain with my eyes. I just walked and held my breath like everyone else, ready for something to bump up against my leg.

I felt the guy next to me shudder. He was a big fellow I'd never seen before. We joined hands and started moving along. "Jesus Christ," he said, shaking his head back and forth. "If that boy's out here, I hope we find him soon, but I don't mind saying I'd rather not be the one that does."

Every once in a while somebody would jolt abruptly, and the line would stop moving as he reached down to see what he'd hit. But it was always a sunken log or good size boulder half-buried in the sand, and we'd start up again, hearts pounding against our ribs.

By daybreak we were all exhausted, and more people from town had been notified and showed up to relieve us. It went on for two days and nights, and nothing ever came of it. I watched Pete grow gradually more withdrawn until he couldn't stand it any more and simply went home. Maura never did—she stayed through all of the searching, even when the scuba men came. She stayed after they left later that week, and I'd see her down there every time I went by, walking the length of the shore and down toward the spillway.

One night I went down to talk to her. She'd stopped walking and was just sitting on the grass above the spillway, staring down into the water as it curved over the smooth cement rim. I don't think she'd even heard my truck coming, she was so lost in her thoughts.

"Maura!" I called as I came up on her. She looked around, gave me a smile, and stretched out her legs in front of her like she was going to get up. Then she gave me a sad smile and motioned for me to join her. I sat down next to her.

"It's strange," she said, "but I feel kind of peaceful now." I was going to ask what she meant but thought better of it and let the silence unwind. After a moment, she continued. "When it first happened, I thought if I came down here and looked for him, really looked for him, I'd find him. I half expected him to just come walking out of the woods as alive as the day he was born, and I'd have to hug him and then smack him on the jaw for scaring the hell out of us. But anymore, I know I was just trying to pretend he'd never died in the first place. Now I know he's dead. I can just feel it, in here," she said, and she thumped on her chest with her knuckles.

"Pete and me, we haven't had much to talk about these three years since the divorce," Maura said. I wanted to stop her from talking, and I almost put my arm around her, but I didn't. "Pete called last night to say he's starting to change his mind after all, to think maybe Jack just pulled a stunt with all this, that he wanted to take off for a while and so he pulled a stunt. It's funny, because I thought I was the one who couldn't accept that my son is gone. Here I am finally realizing Jack ain't coming back—that he's really dead—and Pete's going the other direction."

"You two never could get an agreement going, could you?" I said.

She paused a moment. I hadn't meant for that to be a question, really, not the kind you get an answer to, but Maura seemed to be thinking on it. She shook her head slowly, the smile on her face just thin enough to show what was underneath, and she got to her feet.

"We agreed on something once," she said. "We really did. But even that's gone now."

I watched her walk back toward the shore, but instead of continuing on down the waterfront toward the woods, like I expected her to, she turned and went over the bridge and toward her truck. She backed out, sent one more look my way, and drove off. I had a feeling she wouldn't be back to the lake for a long time, maybe never.

Pete has sold the boat and he called just the other day to say he's moving off the lake next month. He said he knows that the sheriff routinely sends a patrol to scout the lake and waterway, but they haven't found so much as a piece of Jack's clothes to confirm that he actually drowned in the lake. Pete says he's read that a body will almost always show up, and so that's proof Jack may not have drowned after all. He never asks what I think, and that's a relief because I don't know what I'd say to him anymore. So I just listen.

But I can't help it, I keep seeing this picture in my mind of that old canoe I caught a glimpse of during the search. You probably wouldn't see it if you didn't know it was there, lying in a hollow where I'd last left it years ago, weeds sticking up through its rotten wood belly.

History

Ross Burton's life imploded one afternoon this winter. I know. I was there to see it happen. I felt a little guilty at first—I was so glad it wasn't me—and the truth is I wouldn't wish his troubles on anybody. When you see pain that close up, it has a way of reminding you that your own problems aren't so bad. Up to the point it happened, Ross was the butt of a lot of jokes around the office, but that all came to a halt when things got serious. We didn't have fun at his expense after that.

It started with the man who arrived one morning and asked for the office of Ross Burton. When Alicia, the receptionist, said he wasn't in, the man asked when Ross was expected back.

"Within the hour," she told him. "He's gone to a meeting. Is there anything I can help you with?" I was standing nearby—actually I'd been talking with Alicia—and I noticed the man's face twitch slightly at the question, a smirk rippling beneath his features.

"No," he said, a little too smoothly. "Thank you. Do you mind if I wait?"

Alicia gestured to the chair outside Ross' office. "Be my guest," she said. I thought as I looked him over that nobody would want this guy as a guest. I had no idea what he was there for but I could tell it wasn't to spread good cheer.

I didn't get much work done in the intervening hour. From my desk I could see him in the chair outside Ross' office, sitting impassively in his dark suit, moving only occasionally to clean his thick glasses or to reach inside his jacket and check his inside breast pocket. I tried to concentrate on the chart I was supposedly producing on second quarter returns but it was like having a person stand in front of you as you tried to read the newspaper—distracting even though they might say nothing at all.

I heard Ross' voice coming up the hall about three p.m. and I stepped out from my office. I moved a bit too quickly—my chair banged against the wall behind me as I rose and the man in the dark suit glanced my way, startled out of his private reverie. I had the impulse to rush down the hall, grab Ross by the sleeve before he could get any closer, escort him into the bathroom and warn him to go back, leave the office, run away. It wasn't that I knew specifically what was about to occur, I just had a feeling it would be crushing. The funny thing is I didn't really consider Ross a friend. His personal habits always seemed strange to me, especially the way he would talk incessantly about the Civil War. Ross could quote from memory the troop movements for the Union and Confederate armies, their relative sizes and the routes they traveled approaching any battle of the war. Every conversation with him contained some reference to General Burnside or artillery techniques or some Confederate officer's strategy at Shiloh or the Wilderness.

Ross could be tiresome, even pathetic, but I didn't want to see the man suffer. As he approached that day, walking down the hall unaware of the distress that awaited him like an ambush by enemy calvary, I had the impulse to save him.

It wouldn't have helped. When a process server is on your trail, you're eventually going to get served.

* * *

Ross Burton struck me as odd the first time I met him. You could call it a first impression but that implies a fleeting judgment that ought to be re-examined. I try not to be too judgmental, but like most people, I fail. Usually, when I meet someone, it happens automatically. The first thing I noticed when I met Ross was his clothes. It was a cold January day and I'd arrived for my first day of work a little early. The office manager, Carol, a dark-haired, compact woman of about thirty, had greeted me at the elevator and offered to show me around and introduce me to the people I'd be working with. Ross came in late, just as we were finishing the introductions.

He was wearing a replica of a Civil War-era Confederate officer's overcoat. This was no cheap knock-off. Rather, it was thick gray wool, cut wide at the hip and hanging down to mid-calf. The buttons gleamed in the light, obviously polished to a high luster. There were epaulets on the shoulders. Ross' bald pate gleamed beneath combed-over wisps of hair that matched his long beard, dull brown streaked with gray. The overall effect was stunning. I remember thinking to myself, I guess I'll be working alongside Jeb Stuart.

After I was introduced, Ross removed the overcoat and underneath there was a suit and tie, just like the rest of us wore. But forever after, when I saw him anywhere, even over the board table at a meeting, I couldn't help flashing back to that first moment.

* * *

"Mr. Burton? Mr. Ross Burton?" The man in the dark suit had stood up and I noticed that he kept both hands at his side in a gesture intended to convey casualness. He didn't want to alert his prey.

Ross, ever the unsuspecting soldier, smiled and said, "That's me." He extended his hand and I winced.

The man in the dark suit, in a move so quick it seemed practiced over many years, reached into his coat pocket and removed an envelope, slapping it into Ross' hand instead of offering a handshake. "Good afternoon," the man said, and turning on his heels, he disappeared down the hall.

Ross stood stunned. I'm not sure whether he knew what was in the envelope. I guessed it right away. Ross and his wife Patty had been struggling. It was common knowledge after the dinner party in March when they had openly quarreled. Despite everyone's best efforts, Ross had turned the discussion to the Civil War before the main course was served, and he settled in for a long description of how he'd found a number of artifacts in a forgotten corner of the battlefield at Vicksburg.

"The most amazing thing," he said, his face glowing and his voice slightly hoarse, "was the bullet—actually two bullets enmeshed in mid air. One from a Rebel gun, one from a Yankee gun."

Patty snickered, then shook her bowed head.

"What, don't you see the metaphor in it?" Ross had cried. "It's the defining American conflict captured in a moment in time."

She paused before answering, then said in a measured voice, "No, I get it, Ross. It's just that we spent eight hours that day in 90 degree heat and humidity with that massive metal detector. I nearly passed out from heatstroke. We found the bullets about noon and that wasn't good enough. We didn't find anything the rest of the goddamn day but you insisted we keep looking, swinging that damn thing over little patches of ground, back and forth like there was gold down there."

"We found a brass button," Ross said. "We found it late that evening, just before sundown. It was from a Confederate uniform. Don't you remember?"

The room got quiet then, and we were all looking at Patty. It was clear she resented spending every summer vacation tramping across the fields bordering Gettysburg, Manassas, and Fredricksburg, strapped to a mammoth metal detector that swung out before her like an elephant's trunk as Ross directed her in his search for artifacts from battles fought over a hundred years ago. That was, of course, just the tip of the iceberg. In weak moments I would sometimes try to imagine their lovemaking, wondering whether Ross insisted she dress up first as a Southern belle, complete with corset and layers of skirts which he could then remove while muttering phrases in the accent of a Southern aristocrat.

Patty left the table. My wife Sarah followed her into the kitchen. The party lurched ahead after that and people cleared out quickly after the meal. I think most of us understood it would just be a matter of time before Patty mounted her final offensive.

But as Ross stood there that day, the thick white envelope drooping in his hand, I felt real pity for the man. If he'd been served with divorce papers, as I suspected, they'd be asking for unconditional surrender. Maybe Patty had finally figured the only way to get him to pay any real attention to their marriage was to make it history.

* * *

"Can I get you anything?" I asked Ross. We were in his office. He was sitting down—my suggestion—the contents of the envelope laid out before him on his desk. They were divorce papers all right, a thick sheaf that included a restraining order signed by a judge and neatly stapled to the top of the stack.

Ross' face was colorless. He looked up at me, his eyes blank but beginning to fill with distress. "I guess I could use a drink," he said.

"Okay, I'll get you something," I said. It dawned on me as I stood at the water cooler that he really needed a scotch or something—and maybe that's what he meant—but there was no convenient supply. I brought him the water and he took it from me but made no move to drink it. He held the cup before him and stared down at the papers again, as if to try once more to understand ancient glyphs on a stone tablet half buried in the sand.

"Look, Ross, is there anybody you ought to call?" I said. "Do you have a lawyer?"

He shook his head slowly, looking up at me again. "Never had any need for one. Do you think it's a good idea?"

"Sure. I mean, having to call a lawyer usually means you're in a tight spot, and from the looks of things . . ." my voice trailed off, and I didn't want to state the obvious. "Look, Ross, you're going to need some help. That's a restraining order there, you realize."

He looked at the paper but I could tell he wasn't taking much of it in.

"Ross, you're not allowed to go within a hundred feet of Patty, or the house," I said. "You can't go home tonight."

At this, his face tightened a bit. "What do you mean I can't go home?"

"That's what it says on the restraining order." I pointed out the language to him. He read it slowly, his lips moving ever so slightly. I could tell he was trying to make sense of it all but his brain, probably not used to dealing with the present tense very often, wasn't processing the language.

"Have you got a place to go?" I asked, and even as I did so, the thought crossed my mind that if he said no, I'd have to think of something fast to prevent guilt from rising up in me and causing me to offer my couch as a landing spot.

"I don't know," he said, his voice slurred as if he were drunk. "I could call my mother, I guess."

"She lives in town?"

He nodded again, his hand smoothing the papers before him. His fingers were trembling. It was a pitiful sight, seeing this man reduced to a state of shock.

"But I'll need to get some things," he said. "I'll need to put my contacts away tonight. I don't have my pajamas," he said. I pictured, God forgive me, gray flannel pajamas with tiny cannons and rebel flags scattered across them.

"Look, Ross, you're going to have to get a grip. You can get some pajamas at the store on your way to your mom's place. You're going to have to make do. I think you should tell the boss you need the rest of the afternoon to get a few things together. I could tell him for you. Do you want me to do that?"

"Could you?" His voice was thin. I worried about him driving in this condition.

"Sure. You sit here. I'll be back." Ross nodded, and as I turned to go, I hesitated. "Ross, there's just one thing. Why a restraining order? What's she so afraid of?"

There was a long pause and then he looked up at me and said in a dull voice, "It would have to be the guns."

* * *

I suppose I should have known. The Civil War was, after all, a war. There were guns, and plenty of them. Ross' chief pleasure in life was showing off his collection of bullets found in various battlefields. He had dozens of them mounted in little frames, with the names of the battle sites listed beneath, and at the slightest provocation he'd stop whatever he was working on and launch into a windy description of bullets, battles, troop movements, generals, and shards of trivia collected from a thousand nights spent poring over accounts of the conflicts that so captured his imagination. His favorite artifact was a little leather pouch lined with sheepskin. It was some kind of belt pouch for keeping shells. Sometimes he came to work with it on. We all tried not to mention it, hoping to avoid a lengthy explanation.

It turns out that in addition to bullets, Ross had also been collecting guns for some time, and what's more, he'd become adept at repairing them. He would go to gun shows and conventions of Civil War buffs, and would purchase old guns or replicas of them. He had dozens of the things and in his spare time he would fashion new fittings and replace the worn and rusted metal parts on the relics. He prided himself on detailed re-creations, and wasn't satisfied until he could fire them with some degree of accuracy.

Apparently, the guns had made Patty nervous. Actually, I could understand that. I imagined her trying to deal with all those things in her house, especially after Ross took to firing them in the back yard—a practice that resulted in more than a few citations from the police.

That day when he was served with the divorce papers, some of which he asked me to read to him, I learned he'd gone a step further. The first time Patty threatened to leave him, he'd loaded a rebuilt Winchester rifle, put the barrel in his mouth, and mumbled that he'd pull the trigger if she didn't recant.

* * *

"Ross doesn't look so good."

Carol, the office manager, was talking to me. We were outside on a cigarette break. I don't smoke, but I liked taking my breaks outside and that meant I was often striking up a conversation with Carol or one of the other smokers in the office.

I said, "It's been two weeks since he got the news and each day the reality of the situation gets a little more grim."

"Mmmm," Carol said, drawing on her cigarette. "It's not like I wish the guy any harm, but you've got to admit, he's always been a little strange, with the coats and all. And the saber. You probably haven't seen that," she said. "I think the last time he brought it in was before you were hired."

"Saber?"

"Genuine article," Carol said, smiling. "I felt the blade—sharpened. It must have weighed seven or eight pounds. Ross said it was a replica of the one that had belonged to General Armistead, whoever the hell he was."

"Rebel," I said. "He led the only group of Confederates to break through the Union defenses during Pickett's Charge, if that means anything to you—but his effort was for nothing. The Union closed the gap and he died on the field." I was surprised by my own response, suddenly aware that I had not entirely succeeded in tuning out Ross' historical monologues.

"Well, I wouldn't know anything about that," she said. "The fascination with war is kind of an American thing."

Carol, I knew, was Canadian. The poster of the blue and white Maple Leafs logo above her desk always reminded me of that.

"What about the French and Indian wars," I said. "That's where the British encouraged the Huron to take scalps by offering cash for them."

Carol grimaced. "My family is French Canadian."

"I wouldn't know anything about that," I said.

"Ross probably would," she said.

* * *

I knew things had gone from bad to worse when I came to work a couple of days later and Ross was sitting in his car in the parking lot. Just sitting. At first I thought he might be listening to the end of a song, like I sometimes do myself, putting off the inevitable trek from vehicle to cubicle where there is no music but the keyboard, the telephone, the fax, and the burble of office chatter too muddled to understand. I pulled up and there was Ross, parked in the space next to me, his shoulders wrapped in a rebel flag.

I knocked on his window. His eyes came round to meet mine and I saw that they were red and puffy looking.

"You know," he said after he rolled down the window, "They took Robert E. Lee's house and made it the biggest cemetery of all for Union dead. Arlington. They buried all those dead boys in Lee's back yard."

What do you say to something like that? I couldn't come up with anything. "You want to go for a walk?" I asked. It seemed a better choice than going into the office and leaving him there.

"No," he said, shaking his head and smiling as if I'd said something humorous. "I think I'll just sit here and enjoy the view."

I looked behind me. The building's stucco exterior was badly pocked, rain having seeped beneath the layer of cement so it was buckled and stained. A pathetic laurel tree hung its sparse limbs near the entrance to the back door.

I wondered what he saw.

* * *

Ross had lost more than his wife; he had lost the war. Not in the literal sense. Yes, we all worried that he might do himself harm, and in worse moments, about other possibilities. But in the end, Ross was a gentle man despite his belief that he'd been born a hundred years too late to leap the low stone wall behind Pickett on that muggy day in July and charge up the long hill through the scene of one of history's great slaughters. It was more comforting to him, I guess, because the past has already happened and regardless of the usual disparagement we always hear about living in the past, at least there are no surprises there.

"Where are you living?" I asked Ross one day, not long after the episode in the parking lot. He had managed to regularly arrive at the office but he had ceased to do any real work. It was as though he was unable to hold his presence in the current world, with its cars, computers, and cruise missiles instead of wagons, telegraph, and canister shot.

"I'm at my mother's," he said. "She kept my room just like it was, you know."

"No, I didn't know," I said. "She left your stuff in there?" I was thinking of boxes of little plastic soldiers in blue and gray, a plastic sword and a rebel infantryman's cap—a boy's version of the Civil War. I could see a poster with an illustration of Abe Lincoln reading the Gettysburg Address to a small crowd of onlookers.

"Fourscore and seven years ago," I began to recite in my best Lincolnesque voice, "our fathers brought forth upon this continent a new nation, conceived in liberty, and dedicated to the proposition that all men are created equal."

Ross smiled and interrupted me. "The Emancipation Proclamation," he said.

"Ross," I said. "That's the Gettysburg Address." It wasn't like him to mistake such a famous document.

There was a pause. It seemed to matter, for a lot of reasons. Ross shrugged, the shoulders of his jacket hunched and looking oddly too big on him. "It was Lincoln," he said. "That much we can agree on."

* * *

I could tell I'd begun to get too involved in Ross' situation the day I ran into Patty at the hardware store. The divorce proceedings had been plodding along and nobody knew for sure what stage they were at. All we knew was that Ross had declined to retain a lawyer—Carol's brother-in law had even offered his services at a less-than-going rate but Ross said he wanted to handle it himself. I wondered what it might come to mean for him if Patty took everything. I could see Ross at a Civil War Convention somewhere selling off his precious stock to make alimony payments. Then I happened to meet Patty that day.

Actually, we really did bump into each other, coming around the corner near the plumbing supplies in back of Avery's Tool and Hardware Store. I excused myself, and so did she, and then I realized it was Patty, Ross' soon-to-be-ex-wife.

"Hello," I stammered.

"Well, hi Adam," she replied.

There was an uncomfortable pause, and not knowing what else to say I blurted out, "How are you?"

"I'm very well," she said. "I've been meaning to give you and Sarah a call, really, but I've been so busy. I'm having a little get together at my place—actually, it's not at my place after all. It's at the house of a friend."

"Somebody I know?" I asked.

"I don't think so," she replied, smiling mischievously. It went through me like a shot. "I wasn't going to introduce him just yet, but we're thinking of getting married," and she motioned dismissively with her hand, "you know, as soon as all this other business is out of the way."

I was dumbfounded. There didn't seem to be any correct response. I didn't wish to be rude, but images of Ross shuffling up the hallway at work, his gray coat hanging loosely on his shoulders, kept flashing before my eyes. "Well," I finally managed, "I guess congratulations are in order. Who is this mystery man?"

Patty reached out and put her hand on my arm. "His name is Wallace Brown. I met him at one of those divorce workshops where people who are trying to move on with their lives go to be around others who . . . share their difficulty."

I was sure Patty and Wallace Brown had done some sharing. She had a glow about her that I'd never seen when she was with Ross. Good for her, I thought. I guess it beats gripping a metal detector.

"You want to know the funniest thing?" she said, her voice rising a pitch. She waited for me to respond, so I gave her a tilt of my eyebrows. "He's a history buff, too."

"No kidding," was all I could manage. Poor Ross. I decided right there I wouldn't be the one to tell him.

"No kidding," Patty said. "Except his interest is World War II."

* * *

In the end, Ross did the right thing. We all knew he was going to get fired, it was just a matter of time. The vice president had called him into the office twice in one week, and Ross had returned to his desk each time looking more and more dejected.

Carol, in her infinite capacity for callousness, had even tried starting up an office pool, taking bets on when the axe would fall. I told her I didn't think it was funny, and I didn't offer my guess on the matter, though I knew it had to be soon.

Then, on a Tuesday morning, as I was walking by Ross' office, I peeked in and saw him clearing out his desk. There were several cardboard boxes on the top, flaps open, and he was taking files and cartons out of his drawers and putting them inside. I stepped in the door and he looked up at me. For the first time in months I saw brightness in his eye and I wondered what was going on.

"Ross," I said. "What are you doing?"

"I'm cleaning out my desk, that's what I'm doing," he said. "I'm beating a retreat. I'm like General Lee, heading south, trying to get my army across the river again in the hope I can gather my strength for another try."

"You mean you got fired?" I asked.

"No, not really." He paused a moment while he lifted a painting from the wall, the image dusty but portraying Stonewall Jackson on his horse, saber raised and pointed toward a row of fleeing Union bluecoats. "I just went in and tendered my resignation this morning."

I was relieved, in a way, to know he'd been spared at least one humiliation. After a moment I looked around and saw that he had a lot of work ahead of him so I offered to help.

"Well, that's mighty kind of you, Adam," he said, "but you've got work to do. I'll be fine. I have a couple of days before I leave here, so I'll get it done."

"You're leaving," I asked. "Where are you going?"

"Appomattox Court House," he said, grinning broadly. "I just got word last week they accepted my application to work as a regular in the reenactments they do there every summer."

It was perfect. It was justice. I could see Ross in his Confederate finery, mounted on a horse beside the faux Robert E. Lee, approaching the scene of the final surrender of the Army of Virginia. I had no doubt he'd be able to summon the requisite darkness in his soul in order to play the part. "That's great, Ross," I said, offering my hand. "It couldn't happen to a nicer guy."

He shook my hand vigorously, his face beaming. "Yeah, and in the off-season, I'll work on the grounds of the MacLean House, where the surrender took place, doing maintenance and the like. I think it's going to be a whole new start for me."

I wished him the best, and encouraged him to keep in touch with me about how things went. I thought it might be fun, down the road a bit, to go for a visit—I'd never seen Appomattox and I realized how much fun it would be to see Ross in his element.

When I turned the corner of the hall, I could hear him whistling faintly to the strains of *The Battle Hymn of the Republic.*

Listen With Me

Danny Halloran didn't run away. None of us knew that except maybe his sister, Megan. I believed right from the first that he'd taken off for some better place, just like she said. I expected it, so his disappearance didn't surprise me. All my friends said they planned to get out eventually—leave our small town with its long, dull winters when the banks of snow hardened down and turned black along the row of storefronts on Pierce Street. Megan might have known the truth about Danny all along and just wouldn't let on. Maybe she had to play along because he'd told her beforehand, don't say a word, don't you dare say a word.

The Hallorans had a big house, but it wasn't new. In fact, it was falling apart. I'd gone by plenty of times and always figured it was a fancy place since it was much bigger than where I lived. I saw the columns, the broad porch that stretched around one side, the lawn that sloped gently up the hill toward a distant building I would later learn was a huge garage with a room above it. I always thought it was an interesting house and I had imagined the lives of the people that lived inside to be refined and marked by interesting events.

Then I got to know Megan, and that's how I came to be waiting up on the porch one afternoon for someone to answer my knock. Finally I saw what condition the place was really in. The high windows of the garage were busted out and someone had tacked thick plastic over the holes without even removing the broken glass. Later, Megan told me it was a room nobody used so they never bothered to fix the windows. The front door to the house had a torn screen and everywhere I looked, white paint was peeling off the old wood siding. The sun blazed on the wood at that very moment, and on the columns that held up the roof of the porch. I kicked at one of the columns and to my horror it gave way a little and sawdust filtered down from somewhere above my head. I realized I could have pushed my weight against it and easily knocked it away.

Inside, it was worse.

* * *

Megan was a year older than I was, which seemed to matter a great deal then. It certainly wouldn't now. We struck up a friendship. I thought of it that way for a while, and still do sometimes. Then again, I knew throughout that whole summer I was allowed to get close to her by a kind of invitation that had to be rendered again each day. It was strange, but sometimes I left feeling I'd grown lonelier by spending time with her. She gave off an odd sense of despair, never actually voiced, that was beyond my callow understanding. I was just a fifteen-year-old boy, and sometimes when I looked at her I saw a much older person, a grown woman with deep brown eyes, long brown hair, skin that seemed too smooth to touch. At moments like that I knew I was a long way from really knowing her.

At the time I had only asked out a girl a couple of times.

Mostly those experiences had ended up with both of us exchanging a quick, uncomfortable kiss at evening's end, and
later, there was always the conversation with my friends that
featured invented details. I hadn't awakened to the idea that a
certain person can pull at you, draw you toward her, start up
something inside you that ruins your concentration, or at least
monopolizes it. Megan was the first girl who ever did that to
me and I have never met anyone else like her—soothing and
frightening at the same time. She would sit on the porch those
summer nights with her knees drawn up under her chin, crickets scratching slow songs and the sky black behind her. She
smoked cigarettes she took from her mother's dresser and talked in a husky voice about where she was going to go when she
was old enough to get away from that house, from her mother.
I suppose she was talking to me just like Danny had talked to
her before he disappeared.

* * *

It was a hot summer, very hot. I often fell asleep sweating in
my bed and woke up early to mugginess already gathering in
the air. I'd rise quietly, splash my face, get a bowl of cereal and
eat out on the back steps so I wouldn't wake anybody up. I'd
piss out behind the lilac bushes in the far corner of the yard so I
didn't have to flush the toilet because the pipes always clanged,
waking everyone in the house. Then I'd leave a note. It was
usually the same note, though sometimes I'd change it a little
to make the lie seem more believable. Mom, I would write, I'm
going over to the park to play baseball with Mike and the guys.
I'll be back for lunch or I'll call.

That was it. I'd put my glove over the end of the nailed-
together wooden bat and ride off on my bike before anyone
woke up. I'd ditch the bat and glove in a hiding spot not far

from the creek. Nobody ever stole them. I'd been telling the same lie for so many years I like to think my mother never doubted me. Maybe she suspected but she didn't say anything. I don't even know why I went to the trouble to hide the truth, except that at the time it seemed necessary. There had been a time when I played baseball all day in the summer, living for that and nothing else. The summer I spent with Megan changed everything.

We got together the first time at her invitation. It was the last week of school and I was talking with her as we walked home. She was a grade ahead, so although we knew each other we had never had a private conversation before. We walked the same route home for part of the way, usually with a group of other kids, but on this particular day we found ourselves alone so we started home together and eventually got to talking.

At first it was nothing special. I told her I knew of her brother Danny and she talked about how good it was to think about getting out for summer vacation. She mentioned how she was getting a job as soon as she turned sixteen the following month. We hadn't gone far when I began to feel awkward, as though certain words we said were more significant than they should have been, making the conversation a bit more personal. She must have sensed my discomfort because she slowed down and stopped, looked right at me, and gave a little laugh.

"You're not at all like I thought you were," she said. She made as if to say something else, but didn't.

"You thought I'd be like my friends," I said.

"Yes, that's what I thought."

"My friends are mostly pretty loud," I said, a fair enough description of the guys I hung around with. We started walking again.

"There's that, and then most boys don't know how to talk

to a girl, really talk to her." Megan wasn't looking at me. I couldn't tell exactly what she was looking at, but she seemed focused on something far off. The conversation was definitely going a direction I hadn't expected.

"Talking is the best way to get to know a person," I said. "Not just talking, but actually telling the person things that you think about when you're alone."

She laughed softly and said, "You think more people would figure that out."

We were quiet for a while then, just walking in the warm afternoon and letting the silence divide around us, as if it were a river and we were gliding through it in a long canoe. After a few moments she asked if I would like to come by her house some time. Looking back, I see it was a pretty gutsy thing she was doing, but I could tell at the time it was a genuine, honest request. Later, I would come to realize how lonely she was, and what it must have meant to find someone to talk to.

I was trying to come up with an answer to her invitation when she said, "There's a great place to sit out in the back yard. It's a shady spot up on a hill where you can see almost to the lake. I could make some lemonade and we could sit and talk."

I still couldn't believe she was asking me over. Of course I wanted to say yes. So I did.

* * *

I didn't tell anybody that I'd been over to Megan's house, especially not my friend Mike Taggart. In small towns there are always those families that people talk about, and even if the things people say aren't true the stories get passed around as though they were fact. Megan belonged to one of those families people talk about.

For that reason, and others, I was secretive. And as I got

to know Megan, I found I wanted to be even more secretive, as though I were protecting her and myself at the same time. The things we talked about were sometimes light, sometimes heavy, but I carried it all inside me and I remember thinking I would never tell anyone any of it.

Over time, I got more and more bothered by the rumors I still heard about Megan and her family, even though until recently, I'd passed them along myself. Now the question plagued me. Why did people talk that way about the Hallorans?

One afternoon, after we'd been spending time together for a few weeks, I decided to ask her about her mother and Danny.

"If I ask you something personal, would you get upset?" It was a stupid question. What's a person supposed to say? But I felt I needed permission about going into sensitive territory.

"Go ahead," she said, and I heard in her voice that she was promising nothing. Maybe she knew what I was going to ask.

"I heard someone say your mother is . . . off a bit. That she acts strange, and that your whole family is weird. I heard your mom does these weird rituals out in the back yard." I stopped to gauge her response, but her eyes were flat, expressionless. "So, I wondered if it's true."

"It's because we're witches," she said, her voice controlled. Then she smiled a little and tilted her head. She stabbed out the cigarette she'd been smoking, reaching into the pack she had retrieved from the carton in her mother's room. "That's what they say, isn't it?"

I shrugged.

"So who's the expert on my family?" she asked. "Who's been watching our house?"

"Nobody," I said. "I just heard it said, that's all. I'm not saying you are. I think it's stupid." I was backpedaling furiously now, my face burning with embarrassment over being such an idiot. "I don't mean to get you mad, because I don't even believe it. Anyway, it's nobody's business. I just wondered why people say it."

"Nobody says it," she replied, her voice growing deeper. "You said so yourself." For a moment I thought maybe she would ask me to leave. Instead, she laughed, and reaching up with her fingers she pulled a loose handful of hair forward so the long, brown strands hung ragged in front of her face. I could see her eyes glaring out at me and she mumbled something under her breath that I couldn't catch. Then she brushed her hair away, gathering it behind her neck with one hand, and she was Megan again. "I bet I can guess who that nobody is," she said. "I bet I can guess."

"It doesn't matter," I said. "I don't even care. I'm sorry I asked."

"Well," she said, "something made you curious." As she said this, she slid across the porch step where we were sitting and pressed up against me. I felt her cool skin meet mine below the lines of our cutoff shorts. I was instantly reminded of the difference in our ages. "If I said I was a witch, would you believe me?"

"Sure I would," I said. "But I don't think you are. I don't even know what a witch is. It's just something people say but I wonder if people say it because you scare them." She leaned into me, as if she meant to whisper something, and I felt her breath on my neck. Part of me wished I hadn't asked, but I couldn't ignore the thrill going through me at that moment. I shivered when she put her lips to my ear.

"Maybe," she whispered, "Maybe I am a witch."

* * *

The weirdest thing about Danny's disappearance is that one day he was there and the next he was gone, just like that. I suppose it's always that way when somebody goes missing, but I'd never been so close to that situation before and I couldn't get used to the idea.

Danny had been working at a corner store on State Street, and sometimes I went in there to buy a pack of gum or a can of soda. I knew who he was—everybody knew Danny Halloran—because of what he'd done. He had been the starting catcher on the varsity baseball team the year our high school almost won the state championship, and that was when he was only a sophomore. He got his picture in the paper often enough that I remember my father saying he thought Danny had as good a chance as any local kid to play professional ball.

Then Danny got a girl pregnant. And as if that weren't bad enough, after word got around that he'd done it—and Danny never denied it—he drove off with her one day in his mother's car. They made it all the way to New York City and when they got back a few days later, the girl wasn't pregnant anymore.

Shortly after that he got caught with a bottle of tequila in his locker at school and the baseball coach threw him off the team. That's when he took the job at the corner store and stopped going to school altogether. Kids would talk about him, and about his sister, and about their mother. Most agreed she was a crazy woman even though no one seemed to have ever met her.

I only met her once myself.

I won't lie. I went to see Megan nearly every day because I would wake up thinking about her. We spent more and more time up on the hill at the edge of her back yard, not far from the old garage she called the Barn, where we'd sit on a ledge overlooking the woods that ran steeply down to a street below. We'd sit there and watch the comings and goings, dappled shade around us, out of sight of the house, out of sight of everyone.

I would wake up every day thinking about her and how I wanted her to kiss me, like she had that first time. I hadn't ever felt anything like it. The first time it happened, I memorized every detail because she went so slowly. We had been talking and sharing a cool drink, and when we finished she just stretched out on the ground, arms over her head and her long legs settling in the grass. I felt what was going to happen before it did. My heart raced and then after a few moments she put her hand on my arm and gently pulled me toward her. We lay, touching along our lengths, not talking, and I breathed in the scent of her hair, mixing with the grass and the soil in the humid air. She ran her hand lightly over my chest, and then rising up on her elbow, she leaned over me and pressed her mouth to mine. I felt her tongue move along my lips. My hand reached out and found the exact spot where her hips curved into the fullness of her thighs. There was strength in every inch of her body. She drew the kiss out, I don't know for how long, but it seemed forever. It wasn't my first kiss, but it might as well have been.

We spent the whole afternoon in that way, talking a little, caressing, sharing rich, warm kisses that were so pure and so good, different than anything else I'd ever known. I had no wish to go further, but I knew later, as I rode home, that I would return to that place again. So I did the next day, and the day after that.

* * *

Then Danny disappeared.

Not much changed at first. I arrived one morning and Megan was already on the porch waiting for me. Right away I could tell something was wrong, her voice trembling just a little. "Danny's gone," she said. "He must have left yesterday because I never heard him come home last night."

"Maybe he just stayed out," I said. I could see she was worried. I tried a little harder. "He'll show up later today. We could go by the store and see if he's there."

She just shook her head. "You don't understand," she said. "He's been planning this a long time. He's gone."

I asked where she thought he'd gone but Megan said she had no idea. Still, I got the feeling she knew very well where he had headed. She talked about Danny, the fun they'd had as kids, how much he looked like pictures of her dad. She said that their father had died fighting in Vietnam, how only parts of his body were found after a mine blew him up.

"He stepped right on it," she said, "but it didn't blow up right away. That's what they told us—that it was hopeless as soon as he stepped on it, and for a few moments it was like he thought somebody would come along and be able to help him, but then he realized it was hopeless. Somebody who was there said he just screamed at his buddies to get far enough away before he lifted up his foot and let the thing go off. That's what one of the men said about it to my mother, but it wasn't like that in the letter she got from the army."

Her father had died when she was two, but this disappearance of Danny was a worse loss for Megan. I recalled a conversation we'd had early in the summer about Danny's plans to leave town—something they had talked about often. "I want him to take me with him when he goes," she had said. I asked what she meant and she told me he had this dream of living in a cabin in the mountains. He was going to build it himself, she said, and when it was finished he would write to her and she could come move in.

"That's a great dream," I said.

"He means it," she shot back. "It's not a dream, like some

people talk about things they know they're never going to do. He's going to do it."

So there we were, together on a summer morning like all the others, but Danny had finally taken off and I knew things would be different. Looking back now, I believe she knew he hadn't gone off to some plot of land nestled in a range of nameless mountains. We were quiet for a while, and then I thought she was crying, but I was wrong. She turned toward me, looked me in the eye, and then she put her arms around me right there on her porch in broad daylight. I felt her breasts press against me as she buried her face in my neck.

"Just let me hold you," she said, "Okay? You don't mind?"

"I don't mind," I said.

* * *

I could never quite forget that Megan was older than I was, as if it were somehow a forbidden thing, though it did seem to matter less as time went on. She was more lonely than ever after Danny went away, and her need for companionship seemed more urgent. Perhaps she desperately wanted to tell somebody that she knew where Danny had really gone; maybe she just wanted to tell me. Keeping a secret like that could be terrible. But she never said more about it. We talked about other things.

Because I was spending so much time with her, my friends figured it out and before long their taunting took on a vicious tone. I didn't care, even when they called her a witch and a slut—about the extent of their vocabulary—because it only made me more convinced she deserved a friend. I wanted to give that to her because nobody else would.

And then there was the fact that after my first taste of real contact, I seemed to need as much as I could get.

We were easy together, growing more comfortable when

there was silence between us for a while, even a long silence.
We could sit that way for hours, out on the hill, cars cruising
along below us, a canopy of cool green leaves casting shade
around us. I didn't mind at all that she was older, or even if
she was a witch, whatever that meant, or if her mother was
crazy. I certainly didn't mind the warm, wet kisses, the feel of
her against me, or the secrets that we carried between us like
a delicate body that was neither mine nor hers but something
we created by touching.

When she did talk, it seemed I was the only other person on
earth and she had too much to say. I know she missed Danny.
The summer wound on and August arrived, and he still hadn't
called or written to her. When she talked about it, I could hear
an edge of panic in her voice that hadn't been there at first.

"I don't know why he's doing this," she said one afternoon.
We were sharing a can of warm soda, sitting in the cool grass
of the hill, the air hot and stifling. "He promised me once that
when he left he would call and let me know where he was. He
said he'd call when he was set up and I could come live with
him, get away from this stupid town and all the stupid people.
I hate them. Sometimes I really hate them. I wish he'd call."

"He will," I said. "If he promised, then he'll call."

Megan looked at me, and I felt suddenly like a kid.

"You don't know shit," she said, and she got up and walked
a few steps away before turning to face me again. "You don't
know what you're saying. You can't imagine what it's like living in this house."

I wasn't sure what to say. I thought about leaving, maybe
getting on my bike quietly and heading off before I said something else that made things worse. She was looking up at the
patched windows of the Barn, and a look came over her face
that made me afraid. What was she thinking? I wanted to

know, and I didn't. But still I made no move to leave. Looking back on it now, maybe she was trying to tell me right then but I just didn't get it. Then the moment passed, and she was herself again.

"I'm sorry I said that," she said. "I didn't mean it."

"It's nothing," I said.

"You're about the only friend I've got," she said, her voice was softer now, apologetic. "You listen to me when I sound like a nut and you never seem to mind if I don't make sense." She sat down again next to me and took my hand.

"Danny's going to call," I said. "If he said he would, then he'll call."

* * *

The next morning when I knocked on her front door, Megan's mother answered. It had never happened before that she came to the door, and it caught me off guard. She opened the door, looked at me, and smiled.

"You're here for Megan," she said. It wasn't a question. Her voice was soft and deep, like her daughter's. Mrs. Halloran had the same brown eyes and hair, but she looked like life had roughed her up a bit. I found myself a little shocked to realize she knew just what was up with us. And she surely did. I could tell from the look she gave me, and from her tone of voice. It wasn't threatening, just an acknowledgment in words and gestures.

"Why don't you come in," she said, and held the door wide for me.

"I could wait out here," I said.

She frowned, and in a voice even deeper said, "C'mon now, why don't you come inside and let me get you a cold drink?"

I went inside. The shades were drawn in every room and I

had the feeling I was going underground, into a cave marked with the symbols of a people long since vanished. As my eyes adjusted to the light I could make out a hallway off to my left, with rooms off each side, and an ornate banister along a flight of stairs going up the second floor. Knickknacks covered every surface and every wall was hung with framed art. The effect was overwhelming. Mrs. Halloran walked slowly toward the kitchen. She stopped in the entryway and motioned for me to join her.

"Megan's in the shower," she said. "I think she's expecting you. Are you a little early today?"

My secret was not a secret, I realized again. I nodded. "A little, I guess."

"That's okay," she said. "I know how much Megan enjoys your company these summer mornings. She's told me so much about you." Mrs. Halloran was barefoot and wearing a red and gold house dress of some ancient vintage, but her face was made up and her dark hair was gathered into a loose braid that swung behind her as she opened the refrigerator. She reached in and removed a pitcher, then got two glasses and brought them to the table, motioning for me to sit down. As I did so, she pulled slowly on the shade and let light in through a narrow window so it landed on the table in a bright splash. She poured us each a glass of lemonade and I saw that her hands were very much like Megan's—small and slender, with perfect nails.

I was afraid she was going to ask me questions about myself. I didn't know what I was going to say. I could hear the sounds of Megan moving around upstairs. I hoped she was dressing quickly and getting ready to come down.

Just then her mother did something that surprised me. She reached out and touched the back of my hand, just like that, and when I looked up, she was staring in my eyes.

"She misses her brother," Mrs. Halloran said. "I suppose she's told you that. She misses him terribly. It's nice that she has somebody to talk to about it."

The intimacy of the moment was almost too much for me. I was sitting with a woman I had never met, the mother of a girl who was holding me captive, and whom I thought I was hiding from the world. This was a woman some people said was deranged, and after only a couple of brief exchanges she was going right to the heart of everything.

"I told Megan that maybe he'll call soon." I said this because it was the only response I could make. Mrs. Halloran smiled at me, a smile so pained I couldn't bear it and looked away. I knew that whatever people said about her, it wasn't true she was crazy. It was more like she was suffering from some terrible sadness, and you could read it in her every motion.

"I hope you're right," she said.

* * *

What happened next still haunts me, and it's been years now but I can't forget how it felt. I found out the truth from a friend whose father was a cop. Afterwards, I never talked to Megan again, nor she to me. When I saw her, she was distant, cold— not in a cruel way, but I knew better than to approach her. It was like we would never have another thing to say to each other and it was agreed on, without any anger or regret.

It was Megan who found Danny, his body hanging from a crossbeam in the Barn. It had been many days since his disappearance and my friend told me that the evening before, his father was on patrol and had been called to the Halloran's house. He was the first cop to arrive. My friend had listened to his father telling the details of the scene to his wife late at night in their kitchen. After my friend relayed those details to me, I was not sure what to say or do. I only knew that in that moment, my time with Megan had ended.

Danny had run away, but not very far. According to my friend's story, Danny left a note in which he said he hoped people were proud of themselves for acting so cruel to him and to his family. He apologized to his sister for what he was about to do. Danny also wrote that he wasn't the only one who'd had to find a doctor in New York—he'd heard about this doctor from one of the girls at school who got pregnant from the gym teacher, Mr. Avery. He said everybody in the whole town could go to hell, as far as he was concerned, and then the note ended with him apologizing again, this time to his mother.

I tried to imagine it, the image of Megan unlocking the door to the Barn, opening it and stepping inside, the air rich with the smell of decay, her eyes adjusting slowly to the dark. It took her all that time before she had been able to open the door, to look inside. Maybe she was surprised after all, and stood in shock as she realized her brother hadn't run away, that he hadn't gone off on some romantic journey to find himself and make his own way. Instead, he'd written out a note and slipped it in his shirt pocket, then he'd taken a rope, knotted it crudely, thrown it over the beam and tied it off, slipped the open end around his neck, and swung out slowly over the dirt floor until his arc shortened and he came to rest.

* * *

I would sometimes see Megan around town, at least for the next few months before she and her mother moved out of the enormous, broken-down house. I didn't find out where they moved to, though someone said north to Vermont, where Mrs. Halloran had a sister.

New people moved in, despite the horrible story of Danny, which I'm sure they must have heard. They razed the Barn, put siding on the house, and installed new windows. They replaced the rotted pillars that held up the front porch. It looked neat and clean when they were finished, almost like a whole different house.

For a while I used to climb the hill from the busy street below, hoping no one was home to see me, and wander discretely back to the spot where I used to sit with Megan in the grass many afternoons, the shade trees rustling overhead and the soothing sound of cars on the street below. I'd lie down, close my eyes, and listen to the cars going by and sound of birds busy in the trees above. I would try to imagine that she was there beside me, not touching but so close that I could reach out and put my hand on her arm or brush the hair back from her face.

Shots

I'm not going back there. You can tell her whatever you want to, I say to Johnny, but nothing can make me stay one more day in that trailer, not so long as Clay is around. I don't care what Momma says, I don't care if she says she'll beat me or whatever. Clay is crazy. He said he was going to stop acting crazy but I know he won't. He never will. He always forgets and then he's back to his old self again, screaming at Momma, hitting us around. You don't want him to just keep on doing that, do you? I ask Johnny but he won't listen. He's all crying and his nose is running and he doesn't even have his boots on. He's standing in the snow up to his knees, grabbing on my coat sleeve and begging me to come back to the trailer, but I'm not going to. I'm older than Johnny. I'm twelve. I can leave if I want to.

Get off me, Johnny, I say, and I try to get him loose, shake his hand away, and he slips and falls in the snow, and now I'm feeling bad about it so I help him up. He's got snow all down his back and neck so I try to brush it off. You got to come back, he says, you just got to. I know he means I can't just go and leave him and Momma there, but there's something I've got to do. It's dangerous with Clay around. I remember the day the policemen came because he was beating Momma up and they put the handcuffs on him and dragged him out to the car. The lights were flashing everywhere on the snow and the radio kept coming on loud until a policeman came outside and picked up the microphone. He started using all these code words but I knew he was saying they had gotten Clay in handcuffs and they didn't need more cars to come. Then he went back inside and I stood on the steps so I could keep an eye on Clay in the back of the car. Momma once told me people can't get out of those cars because they don't have handles on the inside, but I know Clay. I know he could get out if he wanted to. He looked huge inside the car, like it was way too small for him. He was just staring at me from the back seat until the window got foggy and I couldn't see him anymore. He knew it was me that called the police from Mrs. Perry's trailer. Even though I couldn't see him, I knew he was still staring at me, so I went inside. That's when I heard Momma say, no, this gun is registered to me, and then one of the policemen asked her if there were other guns in the house. She said no. She didn't tell him about the rifle she keeps in the closet with the brooms and stuff. I was going to tell the policeman, I wanted to tell him, but I didn't. I thought I might need that gun some day. I might need to use that gun.

I was hoping that would finally be the day they would take Clay away for a long time, maybe forever. Maybe when he got out he wouldn't be interested in Momma any more. Things could get back to normal. The three of us could get along fine, or it would even be okay if Momma found somebody else, like that fellow she called Harley. That wasn't his name, but he rode a big old motorcycle so she called him that. He was different than Clay. I liked him. I used to hear him coming on his motorcycle before I could ever see him. It was loud even when it was just sitting there warming up. Harley would pitch baseballs to me and Johnny, and once I really got a hold of one and hit it off the trailer but he just laughed and laughed, even when Momma came to the door and started yelling about breaking windows and all that. But then after a while he didn't come back. Momma never said why and I wanted to ask her but I didn't. Harley didn't come back and then she met Clay. He never notices Johnny or me, unless it's to yell at us, or worse. He's gone sometimes, maybe for a week at a time, but I can tell he's always planning on coming back.

I thought the police might keep him for a long time after they took him away, but they didn't. He came back today. They could have at least kept him until he forgot about us. I don't know why he even started coming around in the first place, but it's too late for that. Today he just came barging in the door when Johnny and me were watching cartoons, and the very first thing he did was stomp into the kitchen where Momma was and grab her hair, and then Johnny started screaming because he saw Clay was beating her head against the cabinets. So I did it. I tried to get the rifle. I wanted to shoot him. I wanted to blow his head off. I would have done it, too, but he caught me before I could get the rifle out of the closet. He threw me across the trailer, but I landed on the sofa and it didn't hurt too bad. Then I just wanted to get out of there, and I knew I should take my brother. C'mon, Johnny, I said, but he didn't want to go. I got my coat. C'mon, I said again. Clay was holding the rifle and he was back in Momma's face. Johnny was so scared, I don't think he could move. He sat there holding on to the leg of the table and his pants were all wet. So I just left. I had to get outside.

I went out across the field, up to where the trees begin, and sat down. I watched the trailer. I was going to go over to Mrs. Perry's, but I knew the police would probably do what they did before, come and put Clay in the car and take him to the jail for a while, but not for long enough. He'd come back again and just be meaner than ever. Maybe if they fought it out, him and Momma, then he'd leave and I could try to convince her to get rid of him the same way she got rid of Harley. Whatever way she did that, it might work again. That's what I was thinking when all of a sudden I heard Momma's voice screaming something, I couldn't tell what, and then the rifle went off. Then twice more. The door opened up and Clay came out, got into his truck, slammed the door, and drove up the road. I watched until he was all the way gone, past the bend in the road. I thought about going in, and then I thought maybe he'd done it, maybe he'd really killed them, Momma and Johnny. I couldn't hear anything, and I started seeing pictures in my head of the two of them all shot up in the trailer, and I couldn't go in. But then Johnny came out a few minutes later, bawling his head off. He knew I'd be up here by the trees because that's where we always come to sit and wait while Momma's making dinner.

So now he's up here trying to make me come back down and help Momma. I've got him all brushed off now so there's no more snow on him, and I put my coat on him because he's shivering and the skin on his arms is wet, but he's still begging me. He says Momma's hurt, but not too bad. He didn't shoot her, Johnny says, he just shot at the ceiling, and then he hit her with the rifle. She's cleaning up her face in the bathroom, he says. She'll be okay, I tell him. Johnny looks scared worse than he's ever been, so I tell him I've got to go do something and I want him to go back in and take care of Momma. I'm going to walk into town and see one of those policeman, to ask him why he let Clay come back. I want to do it in person, tell him how Clay came back and was shooting up our trailer. I'm going to tell him they better go get him and keep him in jail this time. And if he won't listen, I'll tell him about the rifle, and how I mean to use it if I see Clay drive up one more time in that ratty old truck of his.

Box of Frowns

I cannot remember the name of the street. It's been many years. Even though my mother drove me along it many times, I never bothered to learn what it was called. Train tracks ran alongside and then bent away toward the east edge of town. Elms grew into a thick canopy so that as my mother steered the car forward it felt as though we were going underground to someplace cool and welcoming. When I was very young, I used to strain in my seat to catch a glimpse above the door panel of the trees and the tracks beyond. Later, when I could more easily see out the windows, I would occasionally catch glimpses of trains passing.

I recall one occasion when a train came alongside, listing and clacking loudly, and my mother pretended to race it to the place where the road and tracks diverge. She screwed up her face into a fierce mask, hunched over the wheel, pressed the gas pedal so the car surged forward, and then we both broke into laughter together as the gap between street and tracks widened and the noise of the train engine peeled away into the distance.

That must have been when I was five or six, I can't say for sure, except that I was still young enough to be suspicious of clowns. My mother always loved the circus, though on the few occasions when she took me, driving all the way into Buffalo on a Saturday, I couldn't quite understand her excitement. Even then, as a child, I sensed beneath the gaudy colors and flying performers that a circus was a vaguely sad event, a remnant of something that must have once been grand but was now diminished. I remember especially the eyes of the elephants, dull and moist and heavy-lidded as they tromped in their tiny circles. Even the workers, moving at the edges of everything, seemed to pull invisible weights behind them, communicating with one another through silent gestures and glances, speaking to the patrons only when absolutely necessary, and only then in detached voices. All of it was steeped in loneliness and beauty and sorrow, the same feeling I get when I see the old widow at the park who comes to feed the geese crumbs of bread from a brown paper bag each Sunday morning, her hand dipping in the bag, swinging slowly out, scattering the morsels in her wake as the geese waddle noisily about her feet.

Nothing was more melancholy at the circus than the clowns. The last time I went, I could watch nothing else. The trapeze artists, the ponderous elephants, even the lion tamer with his tremendous whip that lashed out from his hand as though a live thing—none of that mattered. I went to see the clowns, mucking about at the side of one ring or another while the star performers busied themselves in the center. I had gotten over my apprehension about them and imagined that they were my friends, acutely aware of just where I sat. While they mimed and played to the people in the front row, I felt they were really performing for me, far up in the top row of seats, the moldy smell of canvas tent and the dust and the aroma of animals rising in the air around me.

I believe now that my mother loved the circus so because it reminded her of some time in her past when she was a happier woman, and young. She rarely spoke about her past, and when she did she often grew silent in the middle of a sentence and ended up not finishing her story. But she never stopped in the midst of describing the circus that came to town when she was a girl living on the plains of Oklahoma. When she would speak of it her face became like a girl's, flushing with color, her eyes lighting up, her smile flashing.

Sometimes, the telling would spark something in her and she would grab her purse and car keys and hurry me to the car. We would drive down the long tree-shaded street to the old man's restaurant, a place that was more a museum than anything else, or, as she once called it, a shrine to clowns.

So it was on one particular day in the heat of August when we went to see the old man. I was nearing my eleventh birthday, not really a little boy any more, and the visits to the restaurant had become less frequent. My mother had been struggling terribly in those days, spending most afternoons in her bedroom with the shades drawn, her body melting into the tangled sheets. I would bring her glasses of iced tea and sometimes sit with her awhile, trying to talk with her. I didn't understand all that was wrong, only that she said her migraine headaches were very bad and that I should not spend my day inside, that I should go out and ply my "sky blue trades," as she called them, a line from some forgotten poem. But I worried about her, and my father never seemed to notice how desperate she really was. She would be up and on her feet, busy about the kitchen, by the time he arrived home each evening. I think he loved her, in fact I'm sure of it, but I don't think he was aware of how fragile her hold was in those days.

On the morning in question my mother had been up early,

seeing my father off to work, and by the time I came down to breakfast with the sleep still heavy in my eyes, it was nearly noon.

"You're a lazy one this morning," my mother said. "I thought I was going to have to send the firemen upstairs to wake you with a hose."

There was no bowl set out for me, something to which I was accustomed. The table had been cleared already. My mother was dressed in a light cotton skirt and yellow blouse, leaning back against the counter, arms crossed in front of her. Her straw-colored hair was done up neatly and her fingernails had been freshly painted with a coat of pale pink. She offered a smile, transparent as a veil over a portrait of a lady whose blank face stares through the viewer toward something beyond.

I rubbed my eyes and looked again at the table, trying to find words.

"I thought we might go out for a bite to eat," she said. "Would you like that?" As she said this she stepped forward and brushed my unruly clump of hair with her fingers, utterly failing to smooth it down.

I nodded my assent. She put her hands on my shoulders and pulled me close for a second, then turned me around and gently pushed me toward the stairs, an indication that I should go get dressed.

I had not asked where we were going. I knew, from looking at her, from her movements and the way her fingers trembled slightly as she touched me, that we would head across town to the old man's restaurant. And so we did. There were no trains running that morning and the drive was quiet in the mounting heat. My mother dialed into a station on the radio that was playing oldies and at one point I thought I heard her humming along to a song, her voice just below the sound of the music.

Before long the great, lopsided top hat came into view, perched on the head of the enormous clown that towered over the restaurant's front door. Looking back, I remember the first few trips to the restaurant when the clown frightened me, a grinning Colossus to a little boy. His heavy smile, with its garish mouth painted up at the edges, didn't seem entirely like the expression of laughter, though I could never quite put my finger on what was off. He was so big I could see him from far away, first his top hat and then his painted eyes emerging over the tops of the trees so that it seemed he was spying on our approach. Walking beneath his outspread legs into the foyer of the restaurant conjured up entry to some grand circus tent, although without the smells of the elephants and the hollow-faced circus workers sweeping up the walkways or waiting for someone to buy a Sno-Cone at their stand.

"Will Mr. Comstock be here?" I asked my mother as we pulled into the parking lot.

"Of course he will," she said. "This is his restaurant, you know that. He's always here." She smiled at me, her face still a mask, but I could see in her movements a sense of anticipation, and also a great need.

The restaurant was quiet that day, despite the implied noise of its thousand bits of gaudy circus memorabilia. For years afterward I dreamt of the place, remembering its interior faithfully though the building itself had been long since demolished. In those dreams I was packing away the myriad clown statues, the paintings and framed photos, the display cases full of horns and hoops and faded ribbons, filling box after box but never seeming to make any progress.

My mother entered first and I followed, stepping through the door into the low light, the faint scent of dust mixing with the smells of hamburgers and cotton candy. I can't say how many times we actually went to this place, only that it was always early in the day and we would rarely see another customer. My mother said it was because it was *our* restaurant, and on that day I could tell right away that no one else was there because the room was terribly quiet, already far along in its transformation from restaurant to museum.

My mother had known the old man for a long time. I would say they were friends, which was unusual since I did not know my mother to have any other friends. Perhaps, in a time before her troubles, before the doctors and the long afternoons of sleep and crying, when she was a young woman—maybe before I was born she had been able to make friends. But Mr. Comstock, the inscrutable man who owned the restaurant, was the only person with whom she talked freely, the only one who could make her laugh out loud. There was never any other man, not even my father, who could make her forget herself like he did, if only for a little while.

I was becoming aware of all this at the time, and so I watched closely as we entered the restaurant, feeling the warmth growing in her as she became ever so slightly more animated. She had taken a moment to straighten her skirt and I could see her check her reflection as we passed through the foyer.

Mr. Comstock was sitting at the lunch counter when we entered and he greeted us with a casual wave and a smile.

"Hello, Mrs. Burke," the old man said. "And hello to you too, Buffalo Billy. How are you on this fine morning?" His voice was deep and sonorous, as though he were announcing in center ring the arrival of the next main attraction. As he spoke, he did what he always did upon our arrival. He extended his hand, and I saw that my mother's hand had already risen to meet his, as if involuntarily, as if drawn by an invisible thread from her side, ever so slowly up until he caught her palm delicately and lifted her hand to his lips, bowing, his lips never touching her but coming so close I could imagine the warmth of his breath.

"Oh, Ed," she said and her cheeks flushed, banishing the veil. "We were just passing by and thought we'd get a bite to eat."

"Well you've come to the right place," he said, "but it certainly has been too long since we saw you last." Mr. Comstock did not let go of her hand right away. My mother had made no move to withdraw it, and even as I noticed this, their hands unclasped and the old man, short and stocky with a long wave of grey curls at the back of his neck, turned and shuffled back behind the bright red top of the counter, his gait made awkward by a stiffened leg. My mother ordered without looking at a menu, as did I, each of us having a cheeseburger, fries, and an orange soda.

Mr. Comstock wrote nothing down, and shook his head when she insisted that this time, she would pay for the meal properly. My mother tried to argue but he had already moved out from behind the counter again, wincing slightly, and taking her by the hand again he led her to a booth below the large painting of the clown holding a kitten in his white-gloved hands.

"Will this table do, madam?" he asked. She nodded and slid into the booth.

After he left for the back to prepare the food I asked my mother about his limp, something I'd never done before though the question had always been in my mind.

"Why does he walk like that?" I asked. "What happened to his leg?"

"Well, of course you know Mr. Comstock was in the circus," she said.

"He was a clown."

"He wasn't always a clown," she said, her voice growing softer. I could hear Mr. Comstock in the kitchen preparing our food, but still my mother leaned over the table and spoke in a whisper. "He once was a trapeze artist—a famous one. But one night his partner failed to catch hold of him completely as he came off a leap and he fell to the ground. It was very bad. He broke his back, and in the hospital he almost died, but the doctors were able to save his life." My mother checked over her shoulder to see that he was not in earshot, and then continued.

"They told him he would never walk again, but he was a strong man and he didn't accept that. He worked very hard to regain his health and he proved them wrong. He did learn to walk again, but with great difficulty, as you can see. He certainly couldn't work on the trapeze any more." Her voice trailed off a bit here and I waited for her to recover. "The circus is like a family," she said, "and they take care of their own. So when he could walk again he caught up with the troupe and the manager gave him a job as a clown."

I gazed around the room at the many clowns—paintings, statutes, stuffed dolls, photos in black and white or color, wondering which one he was. There were so many.

My mother followed my gaze and smiled. "Every clown makes up his own face. They're each unique," she said. "Can you pick him out?"

I got up and moved about to get a better look at the clown photos on the far wall. The place was loud with the clutter of images and color. There were so many colors, more than I have ever seen in one room before or since, more than ever were at the circus itself. Every table top was a different color, every wall surface crammed with clown faces, garb, and gear. In one corner an outfit hung in a glass case. I pressed my face up against the glass and looked at the mismatched plaid suit, the elongated shoes, the ridiculous fat tie with whorls that made me dizzy.

The restaurant really was a museum, and looking back I saw my mother, her hands clasped on the tabletop, a look of contentment on her face, and I thought maybe my mother loved the old man, though I could not say for sure. Maybe she was just caught up in the magic of the clowns, like I felt I should have been, but I never could quite trust it. If she did love him, it wasn't something illicit or shameful—nothing like that. He was an old man after all, perhaps in his seventies like my grandpa, and my mother was half his age. Nothing was ever said to make it clear how she felt about Mr. Comstock—in fact she never mentioned him at home and I doubt my father ever knew the place or the man existed. But for the first time I saw something that day in the way he took her hand, and I knew, because I remembered from previous visits, that after we had eaten he would come sit next to her in the small booth seat and tell stories of his days in the circus, and she would stare at him with an expression I never saw on her face any other time.

I could still hear the sounds of our meal being prepared so I wandered a bit further, toward the back of the restaurant where the restrooms were down a long hallway. In this far section the ceiling was lined with striped red and yellow canvas, as if it were the inside of a circus tent. I peered down the hall, then walked its length, going past the men's room toward the half-open door at the very end. Something urged me forward, though I guessed the area was off limits to customers. I pushed open the door and looked inside. It was dark and it took my eyes a moment to adjust. When they did I was surprised to find it was not a stock room after all but more like a garage. On the far side sat a dilapidated trailer of sorts, a wooden caravan. It was hung with tattered flags and banners, painted in swirls of green and blue and yellow and red, a mad rush of color all muted by dirt and grey dust.

The door to the caravan stood open atop a narrow set of wooden steps. The room was still and every footstep I took echoed across it, but I couldn't stop myself. I knew I would go inside the trailer even though it was wrong, an invasion of privacy, like looking in my mother's drawers when she was outside hanging the laundry. When I stood on the bottom step my foot made the whole wooden frame of the caravan creak and my breath caught in my throat. It was dark inside the small space but I mounted the steps and ducked under the banner above the doorway.

Inside I could make out the shape of a small table against one wall, a three-legged stool before the table, and shelves lining every possible space on the walls. There were posters from the circus, mostly torn and battered, and a dull mirror above the table showed my reflection as though I were standing in another century looking out at some other boy. I moved slowly, covering the few steps to the table, and pulled the stool up to sit down, peering at my own reflection.

I could see over my shoulder the outline of a wardrobe. I turned and tried to open the door, which stuck halfway, but I could make out inside a complete clown's outfit. There were the enormous shoes, the front cut away on one to expose a set of enormous plaster toes with red-painted toenails. A pair of orange-striped pants, patched on the bottom and cuffs, hung beneath a green shirt and a threadbare suit coat, the elbows sporting checked patches of cloth. A purple silk was tucked crudely into the breast pocket of the coat. A soiled top hat, the lid flapping loose, rested on a shelf above.

I reached out to take the hat but thought better of it and

withdrew, my hand coming to rest on a box atop the table. As I looked closer I saw the small wooden box was quite lovely, hand-painted in deep red with twining gold leaf around the edges. I opened the lid and found inside a half dozen old tubes of greasepaint, some brushes and soft cloths, and a handful of thick pencils. I picked up each of these things, gently, meaning no disrespect but unable to stay my hand. The paints felt dried out, the brushes stiff as though they had not been used in decades.

At that moment I became acutely aware that I'd been away far too long to claim I was merely using the bathroom. I stood abruptly, hoping I might hurry back to find our meal had arrived and my mother oblivious to my long absence. As I turned to leave I caught a glimpse of a black and white photograph tacked to the wall by the door. It was a picture of a clown standing outside a trailer—the very trailer I was in—his right arm extended so he was propped against the back door. The clown was wearing the outfit I just examined inside the wardrobe, though in the photo the colors were shades of grey. Still, the suit looked bright and animated on his form. I looked at the clown's face and saw, to my surprise, that it was not a smile there but a soft and subtle frown that pulled at the mouth and eyes. I'd seen sad clowns before but not like this one, the face drawn with such skill that even were the man beneath to smile, as this man seemed to do in the picture, the frown would roll through every feature, weighing down every contour.

I stared a moment longer, taking it in, knowing why this photo was not in front with all the other clowns. Then I was out the narrow door and down the steps, moving as quickly as I could without making a loud noise. At the hall again I opened the bathroom door and let it close, hoping it would signal where I'd been.

My mother's voice was the next sound I heard, coming quick and high, a strained, choking sound that stopped me cold. Mr. Comstock said something in response, the deep rumble of his bass voice muted so that I could not make out the words, only the tone. He was urging her to do something and I knew from her familiar voice that she was scared, not of him but of what she was herself saying. I inched closer, toward a vantage point where I could see round the corner of the wall to the booth where they sat. My mother came into view, leaning forward over the table, her arms extended. Another step and I saw Mr. Comstock, sitting across from her, his hands holding hers. The look on his face was kindly, full of concern. My mother was crying, tears running down her cheeks. She lowered her head, looked down into her lap, and the old man said something else to her, causing her look up abruptly, eyes flashing. She shook her head softly and fresh tears cascaded down. She withdrew her hands from his. He left one on the table, palm up, while she reached for her purse. There was a long pause and then slowly, she began to rummage through its contents.

A few moments later she found what she was looking for and retrieved it. I couldn't tell at first what she had clasped in her hand but I could see her knuckles whiten, her hand tremble as she brought it forward and rested it in Mr. Comtock's palm. He leaned closer, looked into her eyes, nodded and spoke her name. She looked up at him, closed her eyes, and her hand unclasped, dropping the item into his. At this gesture, the old man reached up with his other hand and gently cupped her cheek before scooting with difficulty out from the booth seat. I pulled back, not wanting to be seen at that moment, and heard him say clearly, "You don't need these, Laura. There's no good in them at all."

He moved across the room toward a trash bin. It was then

I could see what he had in his hand—a small container with a lid, like so many I'd seen in my mother's top dresser drawer. Mr. Comstock took the lid from the plastic container and without looking back at her he poured the contents into the trash, little yellow pills streaming out like forbidden gems. He dropped the empty bottle in when he was finished.

My mother was drying her face with a tissue. Mr. Comstock turned toward her again and said something I couldn't understand, then went back toward the kitchen in his odd shuffle-step. She watched him go.

That was my chance. I came round the corner and headed for the table, trying to act nonchalant, pretending to dry my hands on my shirt. My mother turned her head and when she saw me coming, she smiled warmly, her face composed and only a redness in her eyes to betray what I had just witnessed.

"Billy," she said. "You were gone so long. Our food is almost ready."

"The clowns," I said. It was all I could manage to say.

She nodded and smiled again. "They're wonderful, aren't they?"

Bones on the Porch

A snowstorm had blown in during the night and the weak sun struggled through the clouds as Matt rose to check the scene outside. The sideways-blown snow, the sculptured drifts and pall of darkness, were harbingers of a brutal winter, but on that November morning he only knew it looked grim that day for any activity except staying inside. Then, as he turned away to head for the kitchen, he caught a glimpse of the dog.

It crouched low on the top step, trying to stay out of the wind, trying to get close to the warm air leaking from the door frame. Matt didn't hesitate. He opened the door. The dog, a small border collie mix, just sat there shivering, leaning away from him, eyes narrow with distrust. Matt bent down cautiously, waiting until the dog relaxed a little before he ran his hand down its flanks, over the jutting hip bones. The dog was too consumed with shivering to make any move. Carefully, he lifted the creature in his arms and brought it inside, all the time speaking gently and brushing ice from its mottled black and white coat.

His wife came out of the bedroom as he walked past, her

hands cinching a knot in the belt of her robe.

"I found him sitting on the porch," Matt said. "He's nothing but bones."

Tracy's eyes were puffy with sleep but she moved quickly to retrieve an old afghan from the closet. The dog lay with its head on Matt's lap, and Tracy draped the blanket over them both, then went into the kitchen to make some coffee. A few minutes later she brought two cups into the small living room on a tray, her bare feet making a muffled sound on the wood floor. They sat together on the sofa, the dog wrapped up between them and drawing in their warmth. His shivering slowed, then stopped, and soon he fell asleep.

Neither of them wanted to move, to disturb the dog's rest. How strange, Matt thought. It takes something like this.

* * *

Tracy stared out the window for a long while after she had finished her cup of coffee, her left hand resting on the dog's haunch, and Matt wondered what she was thinking. Finally she spoke. "How long do you think he was out there?" she asked, brushing water droplets off the dog's ear where ice had melted.

"I have no idea," Matt said. "Maybe all night. I never heard a sound. If I hadn't gone to the front door before breakfast he might have sat there a lot longer."

"He could have frozen to death." Tracy looked down at the dog again and touched his collar. It was old, a worn leather strip without any tags attached. There was only a metal ring, bent as if it had been violently yanked.

"He must belong to somebody," she said, an edge in her voice that caught Matt off guard. "He must have broken loose. But what kind of jerk leaves his dog chained outside during a blizzard? It must have dipped below zero last night. Why would somebody do that?"

Tracy got up suddenly, startling the dog, and headed again into the kitchen. Matt watched her hips move under the faded fabric of her robe. He'd given her the robe as a gift not long after they began spending nights together. She was always cold in the mornings, reluctant to leave the warmth of the covers, and he'd thought it would be the perfect gift. He was right. She had worn the robe nearly every day since. Sometimes, on slow winter Saturdays like this one, she would wear it from dawn to dusk, never trading it for a set of clothes, although sometimes she slipped out of it for a little while.

The dog had stirred at her departure but was soon asleep again, its legs kicking as it loped through a dream, and Matt took the opportunity to get up and follow Tracy. He found her with the phone in her hand, dialing a number, and she held the receiver out to him as he passed. He heard the automated female voice bleat, "Time: 7:42 a.m. Temperature: 5°."

"Well, when we find his owner," Tracy said, her face flushed, "I'm going to tell him what I think of him before I give his dog back. If I give his dog back."

An awkward silence rose between them. Matt knew that the appearance of the dog, and the moments they had spent warming him with their own heat, were not enough to erase the memory of the night before, the things that had been said. He turned back to the counter, wanting to start fixing breakfast for the diversion it would bring.

Soft footfalls came from the other room, and he turned as the dog came slowly toward them where they stood together in the pooled silence.

* * *

That had all happened over a year ago. The terrible winter had ground on, giving way to the usual brief spring and briefer summer of northern Montana. Then in October, the silver maples that lined their street had turned in unison from green to orange to gold. The weather stayed warm during the days, absent of rain and wind so that glorious colors held bloom everywhere, as if the street they lived on were suspended in time. They often took long walks in the afternoons, soaking up the last rays of sun, and as they walked together—he, Tracy, and the dog—sometimes she reached out and took his hand. Matt understood that her hand, with its fine bones and smooth skin, was too light an anchor to keep them from drifting apart, but he held on. As long as the leaves held to their branches, Matt could hope, all through that Indian Summer so unlike any he could remember.

* * *

They called the dog Bones. It was their dirty little secret that they had never looked for his owner, and they kept that secret alongside the others they were already sworn to keep.

Bones had few needs. He ate cheap food greedily, rarely barked, ignored the cat, and slipped outside without ceremony each day to roam the weedy lots near the railroad tracks, always returning at dusk. He began to gain weight and grow younger, more energetic, darting after ground squirrels and running with abandon for the sheer pleasure of it. At night he would lie on the rug at the foot of the bed, although morning always found him curled against their legs, his coat now glossy and soft and lovely to stroke.

Matt had begun to take him for granted when one December afternoon, Bones was struck by a neighbor driving a pickup truck. Tracy saw it happen. Her shout startled Matt, who was in the basement. He'd been looking for a book of poems by Rilke. He'd been so moved by the poems when he'd read them years ago, he'd written comments all over the margins. Matt had been telling Tracy about this moments before as they stood in the kitchen. "You've got to read it," he had said, not knowing why he felt the urgency. "My notes might be a bit distracting but you've got to read these poems."

Tracy was brushing her hair, the brusque strokes belying the fact that she was already late for work. Her hands moved like frightened birds and she seemed not to hear him. "You could just read it and try to ignore my notes," he said. "They're not important."

Tracy grew still a moment and looked in his eyes. It was as though he were a stranger and she was trying to recognize his face. "Okay," she said. "Put it by the bed for me."

Matt hurried downstairs and just as he found the book he was looking for, he heard her cry out in the kitchen above. It was his name she called out and it froze him for a moment. Her footsteps pounded across the floor above him toward the front door and he lunged up the stairs to follow.

Tracy was kneeling on the icy street over the prone figure of Bones, moving her hand slowly down his flank, her other hand braced firmly against the dog's neck, holding it down as the injured animal flinched. Their neighbor, a man Matt knew as decent and who worked at the hardware store on Front Street, stood above Tracy, hands jammed in his pockets, his shoulders hunched forward and face buried in his collar, which he had turned up against the wind. The man spoke slowly in a deep voice, telling Tracy that the dog had dashed out from behind the fence, and that he hadn't been able to stop in time.

"I'm sorry," the man said again and again.

Without acknowledging him, Tracy lifted Bones up. A blot of blood stood out bright red against the snow. She moved past Matt and into the house.

The man apologized again to Matt, offered to drive the dog to his own veterinarian and pay the cost for treatment.

Matt thanked him, shook his head. "I understand it was an accident," he said.

"I'll come by your place later, if you don't mind, to see how he is," the man said. Matt nodded and followed Tracy inside.

She had carried Bones to the oval rug at the foot of their bed. Matt watched her clean the wounds on the dog's snout and ear where the metal of the fender had gouged thick pieces of flesh away. She whispered to Bones as she worked on him and Matt saw him visibly relax. She traced the bones of his leg on the side that hadn't been struck, carefully comparing it with the injured flank. In some places she lingered, her fingers moving softly through his fur. After a while she left the room and Matt heard her crushing ice in the kitchen.

"Help me with this," Tracy said, returning from the kitchen with a makeshift ice-pack. Matt held it against the dog's injured hip as she began checking his body over again with her hands. The dog trembled but didn't struggle. Matt was surprised how calm and sure of herself Tracy now seemed.

Months ago, the last time they had talked about having a child, Tracy had said the thought of being responsible for kids scared her because of what could happen to them. "Wouldn't you love a child so much," he remembered her saying, "that you couldn't cope if something terrible happened?"

"That's part of the risk," Matt had said. "Anything can happen. You can't protect them, or at least you can't always."

She had stared off into the distance for a moment and Matt wondered what she was imagining. "It's too much of a risk," she said. "Too much."

"None of us would be here if somebody hadn't been willing to take it on," he said. "I'd say it's a worthy risk."

"And if something terrible did happen, you'd still be able to say that?" Her voice was hard and he could tell from the way she had said it, she meant for him to reply.

"I don't know," he said. "But right now, I know I can't say I'm unwilling to risk it at all."

That was the last time they had spoken about the subject. They talked of many other things, sometimes staying up late so that the last thing he heard before falling off was the sound of her sleepy voice, but they never brought up the issue of children again. Matt feared it would be too much to mention it now. Even when things were worst between them, when he could feel the holes opening wider, they could still talk, but maybe not about that. And so, as the end seemed to draw closer that winter, he would wait up until she got off work at the restaurant, hoping that talk might save them.

Bones always heard her arrive first. Matt would be sitting on the sofa, Bones asleep beside him where he had lifted the dog, still unable to jump up during his long convalescence. The radio would be playing softly, only the occasional high tone of a horn or crescendo of strings rising above the quiet. Bones would wake, lift up his head, hold his ears as erect as possible. Matt would listen closely to hear the car door slam and then Tracy's steps on the walk, up onto the porch. Bones would already be up to greet her as she came in the door, sliding down from the sofa with a soft yelp and hobbling toward the door. Bones would greet her calmly, wagging his whole back side along with his tail, ears down as he buried his muzzle in her hand.

And Matt would greet his wife, enclose her in his arms,

touch his face gently to hers, brush his lips against her neck.

Sometimes she seemed to brace herself as he came near, as if he were about to apply medicine to a wound. To him, her supple skin was home, and the faint scent that engulfed him when he held her still made his head feel light.

So one night, as she came through the door and he felt her go tense in his arms, he broke the silence.

"What's happening to us?" he asked. He expected a pause, expected her to be surprised, to hesitate, but she didn't pause at all.

"We're coming apart," she said, her voice without color or heat. "We're coming apart from each other." There was no cruelty in it, and Matt let his arms go slack around her shoulders. But he didn't release her. He held on and then a moment later, he felt Bones circling them, brushing up against their legs, drawing an invisible band around them. He hoped, even as his heart sank under her response. He hoped, even though he knew he should not, for something that might yet bind them together.

Something To Fear

Tell me about your family," she said, and for the first time, Julian looked at her eyes and realized that they were different colors. He preferred the right one, which was a soft brown, almost hazel. That's her good eye, he thought to himself, and then he looked again at the left. It was clouded over, and though he thought she might be blind, it felt more like this eye could see through him. He wanted to look away, but the nun's face captivated him and he went on staring blankly, unable to answer her question.

She was patient, and waited a bit longer before asking again. "I'd like you to tell me about your family, Julian. Why don't you start with your mother? Tell about your mother." Her hands were folded on the gouged wooden table before her, the only evidence, other than her impassive face, that there was a human being inside the black robe and tightly fitted habit.

She's different than the others, Julian thought. She's powerful. So many of the sisters seemed to him to be frail and tired, even the young ones. He tried to imagine how it must be, living as they did together in the convent, hidden away from everyone and everything except for this school and the children, and of course the weekly ritual of the congregation gathering for High Mass on Sunday.

Still he had not answered, and Sister Ellen waited. He looked into her eye, at the yellow spike and the thin lashes that held absolutely still above it, hoping she would give up and let him return to gym class. They were playing dodge ball today. It was his favorite game. He was small, a hard target to hit, and many times he'd managed to be the last one standing on his side at the end of the game.

"Would you like to start somewhere else, perhaps?" she asked, her voice calm but also strong, unwavering. "Would you like to tell me about your brothers first?"

So she knew about his family already, Julian realized. She must have read on one of the papers in the file in front of her, or maybe she'd already talked to his parents. He wondered why she was asking him these questions, and what it was she expected she could learn from him that wasn't already written down somewhere.

"I have two brothers," he said.

"That's good, Julian," and when she spoke, he thought he saw the fingers on one of her hands flicker for just an instant. "And what are their names?"

"Mark is the oldest," he said. "He's fourteen now. Richard is eleven."

Sister Ellen nodded, a slight smile crossing her face, and he thought she leaned in a little closer to him. He could see a vein in her neck throb slowly. "Tell me a little about them," she said. "Tell me anything you think I'd like to know."

* * *

Julian's friend Theo had told him about Sister Ellen. Theo was a kid who was always in trouble, sometimes big trouble, but once Theo had helped him on the playground, and since then they had been friends. They didn't see each other outside of school, but they would talk sometimes, usually at recess, when the two of them were left out of the play of others. Theo had helped Julian the day Eddie Czerkowski was punching him on the head with his knuckle. Eddie had Julian in a headlock and was rapping his skull so hard that Julian couldn't help but cry. Other kids stood around chuckling and encouraging Eddie on. Julian tried to get free but Eddie was too strong for him. His skull hurt from the punches, and he could feel a knot rising on his scalp. He felt dizzy and thought he might throw up. Then it stopped and he was free.

When he looked up, Theo had Eddie in the very same grip, a headlock, and was administering knuckle-punches in the very same way, except his were much harder than Eddie's had been. "You like how it feels?" Theo said through gritted teeth. "You like this, you little shit?" Eddie struggled, his arms flailing, but it was useless. Theo held him fast, and the punches came even harder until Julian wondered if they might draw blood.

That was when Mr. Kennesaw, the playground monitor, appeared out of nowhere and yanked Theo's collar, grabbing hold of Eddie's, too, as he came free from Theo's grasp.

"All right, that's enough of that," Mr. Kennesaw said. "I thought I told you about this, Theo. You know better than this."

Julian was surprised. He expected Theo to speak up, say something, tell Mr. Kennesaw that he'd only been trying to get Eddie Czerkowski off of him. Theo said nothing.

"He was helping me," Julian blurted, and Mr. Kennesaw looked up, noticing him for the first time.

"Excuse me?" he said. "How is beating up Mr. Czerkowski supposed to help you, eh?"

"You don't understand. Eddie was doing the same thing to me." Julian's hand went instinctively to his head, where a large, ugly bump was already swollen up. He walked toward Mr. Kennesaw, and lowering his head he said, "Feel this." He felt the large, warm hand of Mr. Kennesaw cover his whole scalp and pause a moment to register the bump, large as a marble. There was a pause, and then the man's voice sounded again.

"Is this your handiwork, Mr. Czerkowski?" Julian saw Eddie's face flush red as he tried to think of a way to deny it. "Well, is it?"

Eddie nodded.

Mr. Kennesaw had made all three of them report to the principal's office. The principal, Sister Dominica, was a humorless woman, pale and slight and ancient, but capable of great wrath. As far as Julian could tell, it was the only emotion she ever expressed. She spoke with Mr. Kennesaw briefly and then turning to Julian, said, "You're dismissed, young man. Please go by the nurse's office and let her have a look at your head." He cast a glance at Theo as he left the room and to his surprise, found him smiling. Julian heard Sister Dominica call Eddie first into her office.

Theo was not at school the next day, or the day after that. When he returned, Julian caught up with him on the playground. He wanted to thank him. He also wanted to know what had happened in Sister Dominica's office.

"It was nothing," Theo said. "You don't have to thank me. I hate Eddie Czerkowski. He won't pick on kids his own size, you probably noticed. I don't like him, and I just didn't think he ought to do what he was doing. I knew I wasn't supposed to get in any more fights but I couldn't help it. I just had to do something."

"Well, thanks anyway," Julian said. "What did Sister Dominica say?"

Theo gave a mischievous smile and shrugged. "Kind of like last time," he said. "She told me how 'disappointed' she was in me, and then she threatened to call my parents, and then she called them. They had to come and get me. I wasn't allowed to come back to school for a couple of days."

"I noticed," Julian said.

"Yeah, and there was something else. I've got to go see a psychologist."

Julian wasn't sure what that meant. Later, after Theo had gone on several visits to Sister Ellen's office, he told Julian about it. It sounded vaguely sinister, as if there were punishment involved, but of a kind he hadn't ever experienced himself.

"She makes you draw pictures," Theo said. "She's really interested in pictures, and what you draw. She's got a million questions. I thought it was kind of dumb."

That afternoon, when his class went to the library, Julian looked in the card catalog. He tried lots of different spellings for the word, but came up empty. He decided to ask the librarian, Mrs. Snell, who sat at the reference desk—always. No one had ever seen her legs because she never stood up, and so the joke was that she hadn't got any legs at all.

"That's *psychologist*, young man, and why, pray tell, are you interested in psychology?" She was a large woman, and Julian always thought she was way too big for her chair. From where he stood off to her side he could see she did indeed have legs. They ran right up to her fleshy backside, covered by a print dress and pressing between the ribs of the chair back as if it might burst them at any moment.

"I just wanted to know about it, that's all." He tried not to look sheepish.

"And where did you hear about psychologists?"

"I just heard it. Somewhere." Julian began to wish he'd never asked her. He hoped her chair might give way right at that moment and spare him further explanation. Mrs. Snell took a slip of paper and wrote the word down, then followed it by a list of call numbers.

"You'll find a number of books on the fine science of psychology in this area," she said, handing him the slip. Then she returned her attention to the work on her desk.

In the end, he was too scared to check any books out. He found several, with long titles and no pictures, and he flipped through the pages to get an idea of the subject. Mostly, it made little sense to him. As far as he could tell, it had to do with how others figured out how to read your mind. It seemed intrusive to him. Why should anyone want to read your mind? Didn't they have one of their own to keep them busy? He put the books back on the shelf and wondered what Sister Ellen might have wanted with Theo's mind.

He thought about it for a long time. He couldn't figure it out. Then he got his turn.

* * *

On a Tuesday morning, just as the kids were lining up to go to gym class, a strange nun had appeared at the door to his classroom. He didn't know her by sight, but immediately he sensed that she was Sister Ellen, the school psychologist. She gestured to his teacher, who came over and joined her at the door. They spoke in whispers, and then his teacher turned, looked right at him, and motioned for Julian to step out of line and wait by his desk. He did so, and the other kids filed out of the room.

When they were gone, his teacher and the nun approached him. Julian felt a tremor go through his legs and he tried to hold completely still. "Julian," she said, "this is Sister Ellen."

"Good morning, Sister Ellen," he said, responding as he, as all the children, had been taught to do.

"Hello, Julian," she said. "I've made a special appointment for us so I can talk to you for a little while. I hear you're a very interesting young man and I'd like to get to know you. I thought we might take a few minutes and go down to my office so we can talk in private."

What was he supposed to say? Should he say, I've heard about you from Theo? He says you ask a lot of dumb questions, things you already know the answers to. He says you always want him to draw pictures. He says you're creepy.

Julian said none of those things. He stood still and waited.

"Come with me," she said, and he followed her out of the room.

It was the third time she came for him when she finally asked him to draw a picture. On the two previous visits she had spent the better part of an hour asking him questions about his family, his favorite sports, what his bedroom looked like, and who his friends at school were. Julian tried to answer the questions but each time he felt more like she was drawing a circle around him, walling him in, and he only knew that, above all else, he had to keep her from bringing the two ends together and closing it off. He didn't want to lie—he knew, somehow, she'd be able to tell if he lied—but she was persistent, and if he failed to answer any question to her satisfaction she would store it away and come back to it later. She never consulted any papers, nor did she write anything down. She doesn't have to, Julian thought. She can remember it all.

On this visit to her office, after she had asked her questions for the day, Sister Ellen turned and opened the drawer of a file cabinet behind her. Julian heard the harsh scrape of the metal drawer, and then the shuffling of papers. She turned back around and placed a pad of drawing paper and some colored pencils on the table. There was also a box of crayons.

"I'd like you to draw a picture for me," she said. "Now tell me, which would you prefer?" she asked, indicating the crayons and the colored pencils. She must have seen his eyes light up, because she pushed the package of pencils a little closer to him. Julian had never used colored pencils before. His brother Mark had some but had always refused to let him use them. Julian could see there were probably twenty or so, a variety of colors from bright pink to a dull, dark brown. Some were shorter than others, obviously the result of much use, but all had been newly-sharpened to fresh points. They sat there waiting. Julian reached out to touch the package. Sister Ellen acknowledged his choice by returning the crayons to the drawer.

She folded back the cover of the drawing tablet and removed a sheet of clean paper. She placed it in front of Julian. "I'm going to leave the room for a few moments," she said, her voice grown suddenly softer, "and I want you to draw me a picture." She rose from her seat and circled around behind him, heading for the door. Then he felt her hand on his shoulder. "Can you do that for me?"

"A picture of what?" Julian asked. "What should I draw?"

"Draw me a picture of something that scares you," she said. "Something you're afraid of." There was a pause, and he felt her remove her hand. "And don't worry, Julian. I won't show it to anyone else."

Sister Ellen was gone a long time. At first, Julian sat unmoving, his eyes fixed on the colored pencils, unable to open the case and remove even one of them. Isn't it funny, he thought, all those pencils there with the drawings locked inside them, waiting for some kid like him to come and pick one up, start letting the lines and shapes come out. He wondered about the other kids who had done this, worn the pencils down and emptied them out, let the scary things come forth. He thought about Theo, and wondered what he had drawn. He wondered, at last, what he ought to draw. Maybe nothing. Maybe I should say I'm not scared of anything, and just leave the paper blank. He wondered what the books in the library said about people who left their pictures blank to show they were fearless. Then he thought about drawing a picture of Sister Ellen herself. There was a light brown pencil, and one pretty close to the pale color of her other eye.

That would be telling too much, he thought.

Julian put his head down on the table and tried to think about frightening things. He tried to remember his last nightmare. He could remember the feeling when he had awakened, the way his breath came in short gasps, and how his mother had comforted him by wrapping him up in her arms, like she had done when he was much younger. He could remember all that, but no matter how he tried, he couldn't recall what the dream had been about.

He knew that Sister Ellen would return soon, maybe any second. He knew an empty page wouldn't be acceptable. He knew she would ask again, and again, and he would have to, eventually, put something on the paper. It was the only way to get out of this room before she completed the circle and closed it shut.

His hand reached out, almost involuntarily, and grabbed one of the pencils. He looked. It was a dark green one, the same color as the paint on his house. So he began there, drawing first the outline of the house, and next exchanging the dark green pencil for a lighter shade so he could sketch in the doors and windows. As the image emerged he began to draw faster. He placed stick figures in the frame, outside the house, each one representing a family member. There was Mark, and Richard, and his mother and father, taller than the other two. He put in his dog, Apollo. He even added the tree in the front yard.

Then, when he reached for another pencil, he came up with orange. It was a hot, bright shade, the color of flames.

* * *

"How was school today?" his mother asked. She was standing at the kitchen counter, her hands busily shucking corn, the thin fibers of corn silk covering her wrists and forearms.

Julian shrugged. "Okay," he said. "School was okay."

His mother paused a moment, then returned to her task. "You're not having any more trouble on the playground with that Eddie kid, are you?"

"No," he said. "Eddie leaves me alone now. He got in trouble for it last time."

"Mmm. I see." He hadn't told his mother about Theo rescuing him, but he had the feeling that somehow she knew. His mother finished the last ear of corn and gathering them all up, she moved to the stove and dropped them, one at a time, into the pot of boiling water. "You know what, Julian?"

He didn't answer, but waited for her to continue.

"I talked to Sister Dominica today. She called here. She said she thinks you're doing much better, now that you've had a chance to talk with Sister Ellen a few times. Do you feel better these days?"

He wasn't sure what she meant to ask. "I felt fine before," he replied.

"Well, that's good to know." Her voice, in a way, reminded him suddenly of the nun's voice when she had first asked him to talk about his family. Julian had the feeling the circle, which he had thought was incomplete and maybe forgotten, was actually much nearer to being closed around him.

"She told me something else, honey," his mother said. "She told me there are some things you're scared of. Sister Ellen thinks maybe you're worrying too much about things. Are you worrying about things?" His mother was beside him now, at the table, and looking intently at his face. "You don't have to worry so much, you know." She ran her hand through his hair.

Julian felt she was waiting for an answer. He didn't know what to say.

"Sister Ellen says you might be afraid of something here, at home. Is that right?" She ran her hand through his hair again and then it came to rest on top of his. "She said you might be afraid of the house burning down."

He didn't move. He wanted to remain completely still. He concentrated on the warmth of his mother's hand where it was touching his.

"You don't have to worry, Julian. We aren't going to let that happen."

* * *

That night, he lay in bed unable to sleep. In his mind he pictured the loose ends of the circle, still apart but coming closer. They moved fast. He knew ships in space could move thousands of miles an hour, and even though the earth was so big, they could circle the earth in a short time because they moved so fast. That was what it was like, the circle, closing around him, with only a small gap left and the loose ends moving very fast.

Outside his window, wind blew branches so they scraped across the siding of the house. It was a familiar sound and he listened to it as though it might be a voice trying to tell him something very important. He closed his eyes and tried to imagine what it said. He strained to hear the words, made of scratches and taps. And slowly, at the edge of the sound, he heard the crackling of fire and smelled the dark tang of smoke.

The Death of Curtis Judd

Curtis Judd died last week at the age of twenty-six. That's how old I am. It was untimely, not a pretty death at all. But I never expected anything different from Curtis.

Dena called, right from the hospital. I was at the cabin— isn't that appropriate—and I suppose Dena thought so too because she called there first, looking for me. She said she couldn't bear to call Mr. and Mrs. Judd, and would I do it for her, just to say how sorry we all were. I asked who else she'd talked to, and when she said, "Nobody else," her voice cracked. So I made the call—I made all of them—to Alex, Sylvie, Daniel. But the first one was the toughest. I mean, I like Mr. Judd, but what do you say to a father who has just lost his only child? I'd hardly said a thing when Mr. Judd just started saying, "Okay, okay, okay. . . ." Then I could hear Curtis' mother in the background, her voice shrill and frantic. He muffled the phone and when he came back on the line to thank me I could hear Mrs. Judd weeping, probably hunched over the kitchen table where I once ate dinner with them.

Dena was with him when it happened. In a way I'm glad it wasn't me. I don't mean to sound cold, but I wouldn't want the

sight of him going over the edge to run on the back of my eyelids every night like some freaked slow-motion movie. I can
see it clearly enough as it is.

It's not like we were even close anymore. Curtis and
I broke up a long time ago—it was all over before he started with Dena. We hardly talked after that last night at the
cabin. It didn't bother me at all when he took up with Dena.
They looked good together, her absolutely straight, black hair
against his pale skin and green eyes.

He never combed his hair—I know because I cut it once
at the cabin. He sat on the dock, dangled his feet in the water,
and I cut with a pair of scissors from my father's desk drawer.
I remember how his hair fell and floated, yellow on the shallow water, speckled rocks underneath. I never told Dena about
making love with him that last time. I mean, what good would
it have done anybody?

It didn't surprise me. The way it happened, I mean. Dena
said he just whispered, "I'm gonna do it," peeled off his shirt
and sneakers, ran right to the edge of the rocks once just to
test her. Then he grinned that exact grin of his and went off.
She thought he was just joking around. I wouldn't have. I
would have known. He must have misjudged the jump, struck
the outcropping below, and couldn't keep it together when he
hit the river. It's a long way down, maybe a hundred feet. I've
looked at it from the road plenty of times.

It didn't shake me up that bad. Not like Mrs. Judd or anything. I gave Curtis up a long time ago. Maybe I knew something. Maybe that's why we broke up. Like the time he scared
me shitless out on Highway 50. But I don't think Dena knew
about that. I don't think she knew at all.

When the River Runs Red

Once look in the mirror told Louis the stings were far worse than he had thought. He stood in the fading light of a late September evening and examined his body closely, counting the angry welts on his legs, arms, and neck—more than a dozen. The hot points that prickled on his back suggested at least four or five more he couldn't see. Worst of all was his left eyelid, which had been stung twice and was swelling so badly it would soon close off his vision in that eye.

This is bad, he thought. This is very bad.

The wasps had been merciless, as he supposed all wasps are, and he couldn't blame them. He'd carelessly knocked the nest from the eaves of the adobe house, where it had nestled between the overhang and the rough edge of a great viga, once the trunk of a ponderosa pine that had grown on the promontory more than ninety years ago. Those pines were all gone now, long ago felled and laid horizontally as roof supports for the adobe houses of San Tomás, which sat on a bluff above the Pecos river.

Louis had been trying to clear the eaves of a tangle of sticks and dirt that had lodged there, using an old rake he'd gotten from the shed. The mass of debris was heavier than he expected so he turned the rake around to lever the mess from its mooring using the handle of his tool. In the process, he had inadvertently punctured the side of the nest, not even aware it was there. The rake handle perforated the papery nest and instantly a sick feeling of recognition struck him. He tried to withdraw the rake handle quickly and that motion ripped the nest from its mooring. It hung there on the end of the pole for what seemed an eternity, then slid off and crashed to the ground, splitting open on the rocky soil below the ladder like the desiccated heart of some great beast.

For a long moment, Louis closed his eyes and hoped the image would disappear, even as the wasps began to pour out, their long, pendulous bodies suspended between silent wings blurred with furious motion. He stayed as still as he could, praying the wasps would simply disperse down the slope below with its dense stands of cholla and stunted junipers, leaving their ruined nest and its contents to blow away slowly in the relentless wind that swept the promontory. The wasps hovered in their silent fury, gathering until there were dozens of them, and then they darted directly at Louis, perched high on the ladder. He dropped the rake and tried to start climbing down but they were on him. He flinched at the first sting and waved his free hand frantically in front of his face, letting go of the aluminum rung with his other hand, clutching it again as another, then another wasp marked him.

They were all about him, swarming his face and head, darting past his free hand as he flailed away. He could feel them land on his calves and the backs of his thighs, each touching but an instant, a ticklish sensation followed by an intense, hot pain. He dared not kick out at them, and with his eyes closed—an instinctive reaction—he could no longer judge in his panic just how far he was from the ground.

Though it had all happened in a matter of seconds, it seemed like much longer that he tried to fend off the wasps. Finally, when a wasp landed on his eyelid and jabbed him fiercely, he pivoted and lost his footing. The shifting of his weight pitched the ladder sideways and it scraped along the rough cement surface of the adobe house, grinding along until he pitched off. He rolled instinctively when he hit, but as he did his left wrist buckled beneath him and the joint turned viciously back on itself. Louis' mind focused on gaining shelter and he came up running for the door at the back of the house.

A low, crumbling mass of ancient bricks lay in his path, the remains of a wall that had once enclosed a patio. Louis leapt over it and the swarm of wasps followed. He nearly wrenched off the rotting wooden screen door and dove inside. The door slammed behind him.

Louis lay on the floor and listened to the wasps pinging against the screen until finally their numbers diminished. His breathing finally slowed and he opened his eyes to watch the one persistent wasp that remained long after the others—apparently a latecomer to the fray who had not had a chance to puncture him and now wouldn't leave until permitted to vent its wrath. It flew in half arcs, banking off the screen at strange angles as if on the very next try it might break through the wire mesh. Eventually, it fell exhausted to the rim of the screen and clung there, its body pulsing.

Louis watched it for a few moments, feeling a strange appreciation for its unwillingness to give up the attack. He lay still on the dusty carpet that covered the old wood floor of the house and tried to gather his thoughts. His skin was on fire all the way up and down the backs of his legs and he could feel already the watery swellings along his eyebrow and just below his right ear.

Louis had no allergy to wasp stings, as far as he knew, but he realized he needed help nonetheless. The first step was to assess the situation. He rolled over, intending to stand up, and realized he'd been cradling his wrist the whole time he lay on the floor. It throbbed and when he tried to rotate the joint, he was answered with a stabbing pain. He rose awkwardly and went into the bathroom, hoping to find a topical ointment that would lessen the pain and swelling that grew by the moment all over his hide. The tiny medicine cabinet held only an old bottle of aspirin, a dried and contorted tube of toothpaste, and assorted other medications so old they bore no expiration dates at all. A faded price sticker on the aspirin read '39 cents' and he guessed it must have been purchased by his mother in a South Dakota drug store, then brought here when they first came to San Tomás on vacation. That would have been almost three decades ago, Louis realized.

There was nothing he could use. This was his family's summer house, or it had been for quite a while. They had visited it more often than just summer, though, coming whenever the family could get a week, or even four or five days, free from their commitments. His father would leave his assistant in charge of the veterinary hospital, his mother would busy herself packing clothes, food, and other provisions, and Louis would help his brother Aaron pack the station wagon. These were some of the happiest times of his life, and as Louis rolled the memories through his mind again he could feel again the anticipation that had preceded a journey to San Tomás—the thought of tubing down the river, red with silt washed from the mesas, and the peace of sleeping outside, meteors firing over the dark forms of the land and cicadas trilling in chorus.

Such pleasure did not last long. Everything had changed after the incident with Aaron and that beautiful local girl, Maria

Elena Escobar. Everything. The events after that point all occurred in Louis' memory in black and white—the angry con-
frontations, Aaron's fight with their father, and then his disappearance. It was four years later when they finally heard of
him again, and it was only because he'd been killed in a motorcycle accident outside Seattle. Louis' mother had never given
up hope that they would some day be reunited, and when the
news came that Aaron was dead, something vital went out of
her. Six months later she, too, was dead, and after that, Louis'
father would never return to San Tomás. Louis went off to college in Colorado, and because of his proximity to the vacation
house, the task fell to him to return there each autumn to perform minor repairs and winterize the place.

Aaron stood accused of forcing himself on Maria Elena—
of "taking advantage of her," as his parents put it. There had
been no police involvement since they were both under eight-
teen; the citizens of San Tomás presumed that Maria Elena had
brought the situation on herself by going off with a boy, un-
chaperoned—a clear violation of the rules—although this did
little to calm their anger. The events surrounding Aaron and
Maria Elena had left Louis' family forever unwelcome in the
close-knit community of San Tomás, a community that had
previously come to accept and even welcome them—a rare
enough gesture in these parts. That had all come to an end,
and now, when Louis visited to perform his tasks, the people
in the village ignored him, for the most part. Only Manuelita
and her husband Pedro, who owned the decrepit general store
in the center of the village, spoke to him at all when he came
in to buy food or hardware for repairs. The other townspeople
were not openly hostile. It was more like he was invisible. Louis told himself he didn't mind that much. It could get lonely on
the few nights he spent there each fall, but then he'd always

craved solitude anyway. What bothered him more than anything was to think of how much the local people had come to
adore his mother, Greta, and how she died still horrified by the
knowledge of what Aaron had done—to the girl, to their family, and to the townspeople. That bond the townspeople had
once come to feel with Greta, and by extension her whole clan,
could never be rebuilt.

Louis roused himself, aware that he needed to seek help.
He hoped he could get down the hill and reach Manuelita's
store, where he might find medicine or at the least a box of
baking soda, with which he could fashion a simple drawing
poultice. There would be ice, too, for his sprained wrist. He
went to the front room and checked outside for the presence
of wasps. He could see none, and quietly, his flesh burning and
his ears ringing, he opened the door and hurried out in the direction of Manuelita's store.

* * *

A pale light played out through the front door of the store and
as Louis approached he whispered a thank you. Manuelita had
not closed up shop yet. He jogged the last few steps and then
halted on the rough wood porch, collecting his thoughts a moment before he went in. He could hear Pedro and Manuelita in
conversation, their Spanish slow and melodic, not like the hurried language of Mexican fieldworkers he had labored beside a
few summers ago. Theirs was the speech of the long-married,
and although he understood only a few words or expressions,
he knew the conversation included many gaps, filled in by the
knowledge a man and woman gain of each other after living
together for sixty years.

Louis opened the door and went in. Pedro was behind the
counter, its nicked glass protecting the few boxes of chewing

gum, antacids, and bandages in place so long that dust clung to the sides of the packages. Pedro made eye contact with him, nodded slightly, and then shuffled his ancient frame back through the door that led to the couple's living room, softly calling Manuelita's name as he went. Louis took in his surroundings. A single light bulb cast a dim glow across the shelves that ran along the walls toward the back of the shoebox store. Loaves of white bread, cans of beans and corn, and sacks of rice and pintos were spaced so as to avoid the look of barrenness, but it was not enough. Ancient tack hung from large hooks on the wall, old harnesses and saddles, metal bits and other items Louis could not identify. An aged cooler sat squat in the corner, humming gently. Louis looked in and saw a half empty box of ice cream sandwiches and some popsicles scattered here and there.

"We did not expect a customer this late, Señor Louis," Manuelita's voice announced, a moment before she emerged from the doorway. Louis looked up and saw the tiny woman come forth, her gently sloping shoulders covered in a thin green house dress and loose silver hair—she must have been combing it out when he came in. Her voice was soft and Louis knew it was as much of a welcome as he would ever get in San Tomás.

"I'm sorry," he said. "I saw the door open and light on. I thought you might still be open for . . . "

"Oh, we are open," she said. "We are always open, I think. You know we never lock the door. It's like I told your mother once, Señor Louis, if you should ever need something, just let yourself in and leave the money on the counter." The old woman smiled at him, and then, as her eyes adjusted to the light, Louis could see she was taking him in and the expression on her face changed. She stepped a little closer, squinting at him.

"*Qué te pasa?*" she said.

"Wasps," Louis said. "I knocked their nest off the house when I was working, and they stung me. Many times."

"Your eye," Manuelita said. "It does not look so good."

"No, I'm sure it doesn't."

Manuelita stepped closer then, and to his surprise she reached up with the tips of her fingers and touched the swollen area on his face, her tongue making a soft clucking sound as she wagged her head. She ran her hands down his neck and arms, her fingers taking in each swollen place. She stopped briefly at his wrist as well, assessing the injured joint.

"You will need something for these," she said, and turned to go behind the counter again. "How many times?" she asked.

"I'm not sure," Louis replied, "fifteen, maybe twenty."

Manuelita stood still for a moment. Louis saw Pedro in the room behind her, listening intently to their conversation but pretending to be fully engaged in peeling an orange. The bright citrus scent wafted through the doorway.

Manuelita took a box of baking soda down from the shelf and put it on the counter, then disappeared into the back room again and came out with ice and a small tube of something—not from her stock but rather from her own medicine chest. She handed it to Louis. "This is for your eye," she said. "Don't get it in your eye, now, but put it on there soon. It will help with the swelling, and in the morning put some more on. It will not itch so bad then." She pushed the baking soda box toward him. "You know how to use this, I think," she said, more as a question than a statement. He nodded. His eye was now swollen so badly that he could see only through a narrow slit.

Louis reached with his good hand into his back pocket and realized that in his rush, he had brought no wallet or money. Pedro was now standing in the doorway, looking him over with his glassy eyes, and Louis could not read his expression.

"I . . . didn't bring my wallet," Louis said sheepishly.

Manuelita shook her head and smiled. "You did not listen to me before, Señor Louis," she said. "You can leave the money another time. Now go and get that medicine on your stings as soon as you can, and keep this ice on your wrist."

Louis nodded and turned to go. Then he heard Pedro's raspy voice. "Always check under the vigas," Pedro said. "They build there for protection and the nests are sometimes hard to see unless you know they are there. Next time, I think you will not forget."

Louis thanked him for the advice, aware the old man was mocking him slightly. He opened the door and went out, nearly stumbling as he tried to gauge the distance off the porch with his one good eye.

* * *

An hour later, Louis could no longer bear the pain and decided a cold shower might shrink the swellings that covered his skin. He had disrobed in the middle of the bedroom, the cool night air rushing over his body as he tried, one-handed, to apply the baking soda poultice to all his wounds. There were some he could not reach, and exhausted, he'd given up on those. In the end, it didn't seem to matter if his ass swelled as big as a prize pumpkin. He couldn't see it anyway, and nobody in town was likely to comment. The application of the poultice hadn't helped much, though, and now he felt that even if the cold water didn't fix the problem, it might at least alleviate the immediate discomfort.

He turned on the shower and let the water run a moment, adding just enough hot that it wouldn't be too shocking on his skin. When he stepped under the torrent, a moan escaped his lips involuntarily and he thrust his face under the water, careful not to let the full force of the shower fall on his swollen eye, now extremely tender. He turned and let the water run down his back, over those welts he hadn't been able to reach. The stream was soothing, and he thought he might stand there until he fell asleep.

A sound startled him and at first he thought it was the wind, but the second time, the sound was more distinct. Someone was knocking on the front door of the house. He turned off the shower to listen more closely. Sure enough, there it was again.

Louis got out and awkwardly wrapped the too-small towel around his waist, cinching as best he could it so it wouldn't fall off. He stumbled over the pile of clothes in his room, and then walked hesitantly to the door, using his good hand to feel his way along the backs of the chairs as he approached. The knocks came again, soft but insistent, and Louis could see a figure standing on his front porch—small, a woman's figure, long hair blowing lightly in the breeze. Manuelita, he thought, but then realized she could not have come up the steep hill that led to the house, not with her arthritis. It couldn't be her at all. The figure waited patiently, aware he was now there. Louis had no choice, really. He reached out, fumbled for the knob, and pulled the door open slowly, forgetting that he was nearly exposed with only a thin towel around his hips.

It was Maria Elena.

* * *

Louis had not seen her since he was a boy. She was Aaron's age, just a few years older than Louis, and his most vivid memory was from Sunday mornings when he and his family would walk down to the ancient church in the center of San Tomás to attend services. The old priest, Father Bernardo, would be on the front stairs of the church, greeting the people as they filed in. He would always reserve a special greeting for Greta, their mother, for whom he seemed to have a particular fondness. "Señora Greta," he would say, taking both her hands in his, "God is so pleased to welcome you to his house this morning." His mother would blush, and Louis' father would extend his own hand and shake the priest's hand, the men exchanging smiles. "Señor Pablo," he would address Louis' father, "you are so kind to grace us with your lady's presence today. And your sons, they are so nearly men now," he would add, smiling at the boys. Once inside, Louis would always sit near Aaron, and together they would silently survey the local population. Their objective was always the same. To seek out, from among the many raven-haired, slender, and beautiful girls of San Tomás, the one who stood out above all the rest. Maria Elena. Louis remembered her there, across the pews, her hair so straight and black it seemed to be woven from threads of some dark liquid. Her skin was smooth and olive hued, and he could stare at her delicate features in profile all through the service and truly believe that God's gifts were great.

Now here she stood in the doorway of this house, a woman, who once was the object of his fantasy, and later the undoing of everything in his family. Aaron never denied the allegation that he had taken her against her will. It had torn their family from the fabric of the town, and ultimately, it had torn them from one another.

Louis was speechless.

"Manuelita called me," Maria Elena said. "She told me you had been badly stung by wasps."

Louis was aware his eye was swollen shut and the welts on his body, even in the low light, must be clearly visible. He was aware he stood nearly naked before her. "Manuelita called you?" he said, incredulous. Involuntarily, his body gave a sudden shiver.

"Actually, she sent Pedro. He came to my home. He said . . . I'm sorry, he said you'd gotten what you deserved when you knocked a nest from its perch, but that nonetheless, you needed help."

"I've gotten help," Louis said. "Manuelita gave me something for it."

Maria Elena nodded. "I know," she said. "But she sent Pedro for me because I have something better. May I come in?"

Louis hesitated for a long moment. The strange yipping sounds of coyotes who had come out to prowl cut through the night. He reached forward and opened the door, then stepped aside and Maria Elena entered the house. In all the years of his boyhood, when he had come to visit San Tomás, he had only seen her from afar. Later, after the trouble, he never expected to see her again. Now she stood in the room with him, no longer the lithe girl on the far side of the church. Now she was there in his family's house and an unspoken chasm seemed to open across the floorboards between them.

Maria Elena was carrying a small shoulder bag. She removed it and placed it on the kitchen table, rummaged around inside for a moment, and then came out with a round, earthen container stopped with a cork. She held it out to Louis and he took it from her.

"This is something special," she said.

"What is it?" Louis asked, removing the cork and sniffing the pungent contents. He could smell mint, and something oily and dark—a complex mesh of scents.

"It's an old remedy," she said. "You are not the first person to knock a wasp nest from its mooring, and you know, the wasps have always had the same response."

Louis dipped his finger into the salve and brought up a small dab of the brownish unguent. It was tarry and he turned to examine it in the dim light.

"It has lemon balm, and yarrow," she said. "Also some aloe and ragweed, some mint. Black cohosh, too, all good things for the swelling and the pain."

"So . . . how much do I use?" he asked. "How do I apply it?"

There was a pause. Maria Elena smiled gently, and Louis realized she was taking in the number and location of his stings. "I will help you, if you like," she said. "I know you cannot reach those on your back."

* * *

Moments later, Louis found himself lying on the bed on his stomach. He could not believe that this was happening. Maria Elena had gently insisted that he allow her to apply the salve, at least to those stings that laced his back and legs, where he could not reach. At first he had been reluctant, and had applied the salve himself to the stings on his neck and arms while she watched. The relief was almost instantaneous. The burning subsided, and although the skin still registered irritation, Louis was immediately grateful for the respite. When he had reached all the places he could, he moved to put some on his eye. Maria Elena gasped slightly, and rose from her chair.

"No, no, no. Please," she said. "It would not be good for you to get this into your eye. Please. Let me help."

Louis sat still and closed his one good eye, then waited for the first touch of her fingers. That touch was more delicate than he could have imagined, just the lightest brushing of her fingertips as she smoothed the salve over the center of the sting, making sure not to spread it too close to the distended lid. As she worked, he tried to work out why it was she who had come—why Manuelita had called her, rather than anyone else. This was the woman whose innocence had been stolen by his very own brother, to her shame and to the shame of his own family. He and Aaron had once been inseparable. They had gone everywhere together. The people of San Tomás had been so friendly to them, taking them into their homes and families when they visited. But the ruination had been almost total. He had never been able to escape the stigma of his brother's actions, yet now the girl Aaron had violated had come to minister to him.

Maria Elena finished putting the salve on his arms and then with her hand indicated that Louis should move to the bed. "I cannot reach all the stings," she said, "unless you remove the towel. I will turn down the light, if you wish," she said. "Please, do not be embarrassed." Louis had been reluctant, but realizing how good the medicine felt, and knowing it was the only way he could get relief from those many stings on his lower back and thighs, he acquiesced. He lay there on the bed, the only light coming from the open window, and found himself overwhelmed with the desire to ask Maria Elena one simple question: how could she bear to be here in the house where her innocence had been stolen away? She worked slowly, applying the salve to his stings, starting at the nape of his neck and moving down between his shoulder blades, his lower back, the tops of his thighs, his calves.

Finally, when he could contain himself no longer, Louis spoke. "Maria Elena," he said. "Why are you being so kind to me?"

She did not reply immediately, but kept to her task. Louis waited patiently. When she did speak, her voice had changed, sounding deeper and more resonant than it had before. "I could not say no to Pedro and Manuelita," she said, "and I knew you needed help. There is no one here in town who still knows how to make this salve. My grandmother taught me how to make it, and I always keep some of it around, just in case Miguel gets stung—which he always manages to do."

"Miguel?" Louis asked.

"My son," she said. There was a moment of quiet again while Louis pondered this, and he thought better of asking more about the boy. It was better, perhaps, not to know. His mind moved quickly over a landscape of possibilities and he became aware again of her hands, now applying the medicine to the last of the stings near his left ankle.

"Maria Elena," he said, his voice wavering. "I'm sorry."

Once again, she did not reply immediately. Her hands were no longer on him and he felt her rise from the mattress where he lay. She moved across the room and put the container of salve back into her bag. Louis rearranged the towel across his waist and sat up. She was looking directly at him from across the room and when his gaze met hers, she held it a moment and then looked away, out through the window and across the promontory to the mesas in the distance, flat hulking shapes in the half-light of an autumn moon.

"No," she said, barely audible. "It is I who am sorry."

Louis didn't understand. What could she possibly be apologizing for? His head reeled, pictures of events long past racing through—Aaron and his father shouting at each other, the racing of a car engine, the last glance of his brother speeding away. Then, too, the accusatory looks he got in the following days whenever he went anywhere in San Tomás, and the time a group of local boys cornered him behind the school and beat him until his head reeled and he could not stand. At the time, he felt he somehow deserved it, and even now it seemed he'd accepted that he should forever absorb the justice meant for

Aaron. The cruel looks, the beating, maybe even the fury of the wasps—these were all a penance he deserved on behalf of the brother he had loved so fiercely and whose actions he could never quite understand.

Maria Elena turned again to him, and her voice came out of the dim shadows of the room. "You see, the story I told was not true," she said. "Aaron never hurt me—not the way they said."

"I don't understand," Louis said.

"He did not force me," Maria Elena said. She turned away from him a moment and looked out the window, and Louis watched her hair stir slightly in the breeze. "I think . . . I thought I loved him. I was just a girl, you know, but I thought it was love. Maybe it really was. Still, when my father found out . . ." She stopped a moment and Louis could tell she was struggling to find words.

"It was my father who told me I must lie," she continued. "He said it was to protect my honor, but I never felt that. Still, he was my father and I could not disobey him—not more than I already had. So I did as I was told. I said that Aaron had forced himself on me, and instead of protecting my honor, in that moment I truly lost any honor I had."

Louis remained quiet, listening to the sounds of the wind flowing over the rounded adobe walls and through the branches of the junipers outside. He knew what she was saying now but he couldn't put it into context, fit it into the events that had torn his family apart. Aaron had never denied the charges against him—in fact, he had admitted his mistake. How could that be? Was he merely trying to prevent the girl from her disgrace? But at what price?

"I needed to come and tell you this," Maria Elena said, and she rose again and gathered her bag. "For years, I have carried this with me, and now I no longer need to do that."

"Do others know?" Louis asked.

"I think they have always known," she said. "There are no real secrets in San Tomás," she said. "That's why I left shortly afterward. I could not bring a child into this world when the people here would never accept him. So I moved to Gallup, raised Miguel there. It is only these last few years that I have returned at all, sometimes in the fall to see my parents, who are getting old and need help. No one has forgotten," she said, "but they no longer speak of it. They treat Miguel like any other boy. He belongs now."

Louis hesitated to ask, but he had to know. "So, Miguel is my brother's son?"

Maria Elena smiled. "He's a good boy. Strong, very smart. He does well in school. He has green eyes, his father's gift."

Louis remembered his brother, the shock of light brown hair that never seemed combed, the pale green eyes and everpresent grin. He tried to picture this image blended with that of Maria Elena.

"Perhaps some time you would like to meet him," she said, as she moved toward the front door. Louis stayed where he was, afraid the towel might slip from his body if he stood.

"Some time," he echoed.

Maria Elena smiled once more. "I know you come each fall to repair the house."

"I'm the only one left to do it," Louis said. "You know, Aaron is gone."

"I know," she said. "I knew soon after it happened." Maria Elena turned toward the door and Louis stayed where he was.

"Yes, San Tomás is beautiful in the fall, but it is also a lovely place in the springtime," she said. "Maybe you would like to visit then. The mesas are covered in blooms and the rains paint the river red as it can be. I think you would like it here then."

　　Louis nodded, and as Maria Elena stepped out through the door, his thank you was carried away by the wind.